SINGLE DAD'S CHRISTMAS MIRACLE

SINGLE DAD'S CHRISTMAS MIRACLE

BY

SUSAN MEIER

MILLS
BOON

First published in Great Britain 2013
by Mills & Boon, an imprint of Harlequin (UK) Limited,
Large Print edition 2014
Eton House, 18-24 Paradise Road,
Richmond, Surrey, TW9 1SR

© 2013 Linda Susan Meier

ISBN: 978 0 263 24022 1

Harlequin (UK) Limited's policy is to use papers that are natural, renewable and recyclable products and made from wood grown in sustainable forests. The logging and manufacturing processes conform to the legal environmental regulations of the country of origin.

Printed and bound in Great Britain
by CPI Antony Rowe, Chippenham, Wiltshire

For Jack and Helaina
(the inspiration for Jack and Teagan)

CHAPTER ONE

"Turn right."

The soothing voice of the GPS rolled into Althea Johnson's car, and she maneuvered her vehicle as directed, onto the snow-covered Main Street of Worthington, Pennsylvania. The week after Thanksgiving, the little town sparkled with the spirit of Christmas. Tinsel connected to telephone poles looped above the street. Huge evergreen wreaths decorated with shiny multicolored ornaments covered the top half of shop doors. Silver bells glistened in the sun that managed to peek through the falling snow.

But as quickly as she entered the tiny town, she exited. The GPS stayed silent so she continued up the winding road and climbed a tree-covered mountain.

Up and up she went for a good ten minutes, causing her palms to sweat as her car just barely chugged through the wet snow. Positive she'd missed an exit, she was about to look for a place to turn around when the GPS sang out, "In thirty feet, turn left."

With a sigh of relief, she braked slowly, carefully. She'd learned to drive in Maryland winters, but she'd spent the past twelve years in sunny Southern California. Her car didn't have snow tires and her driving skills were a bit rusty.

"Turn left."

Braking again, she guided her little red car down a short lane lined with snow-coated pine trees. A huge Victorian house came into view. A pewter-colored SUV had been parked haphazardly in the driveway. A man reached in and pulled grocery bags out of the open hatch. Snow fell on him like cotton balls from heaven, covering his shoulders and back, and icing the evergreens that ringed his property. A big black dog bounced around him. A little girl clung to the hem of his jacket.

Frazzled.

That's the word that came to Althea's mind. She stopped her car, pushed open the door and slid out. The big dog bounded over with a "Woof." In one quick movement, he jumped on his hind legs, his paws landed on her shoulders and she fell backward into the snow.

Cold seeped through the back of her light-weight jeans and Southern-California hoodie. Huge white flakes billowed down on her.

Trapped by the dog—who had his paws on her chest as if he were holding her down until the police could get there—she only saw boots rapidly approaching.

"Crazy!"

The man gave the dog a nudge. The beast bounced off with another "Woof!"

He extended his hand. "Let me help you up."

She gaped at him. His face was perfect with a straight nose, angled cheekbones and the tint of five o'clock shadow, even though it was only noon. "Did you just call me crazy?"

"The dog's name is Crazy. Her given name is Crazy Dog. If she had a birth certificate that's what would be on it."

She laughed.

She came up so fast that she stopped inches away from his nose. This close, she could see his whiskey-brown eyes that perfectly matched his light brown hair.

"You named your dog Crazy Dog?"

He stepped back, putting some space between them. "After the way she knocked you down, I would think you wouldn't be surprised."

She laughed again. Cold air filled her lungs. She slapped her hands together to remove the snow.

"Let me get your back."

The words were barely out of his mouth before he turned her around and brushed the snow off her back and then did a quick sweep over her bottom.

"If this stuff melts on your clothes you'll be wet all afternoon."

Her nerve endings tingled. Her breath stuttered in and out. The intimacy of it should have made her indignant. Instead, it felt surprisingly…normal. This was a man who saw a problem and fixed it. For him, his brushing her butt was nothing more serious than that. For her…well, she hadn't had a man touch her in years. So even that simple brush zinged through her and sent the wrong kind of warmth careening through her bloodstream.

She pivoted to face him. "I'm fine. You don't have to brush anymore."

"That big, stupid dog should know her place." His eyes narrowed as he looked at her hoodie and jeans. "I'm hoping you have a coat in the car."

"I'm from Southern California." Funny how easy that came out of her mouth when really she was "from" right down the road. Newland, Maryland, was only fifty or so miles away from the green hills of Pennsylvania, where Clark Beaumont lived.

"California?" He stepped back. "Are you Althea Johnson?"

"In the snow-covered flesh." She extended her hand to shake his. "I take it you're Clark Beaumont."

He caught her hand, gave one quick pump and pulled back. "I thought you weren't coming until Friday?"

"Once I told Emily," she said, referring to the mutual friend who had told her about the job and referred her to Clark, "that I would interview with you, I drove straight through."

"You haven't slept?"

"Or really eaten for that matter."

"Wow. This is not your lucky day. Things sort of went to hell in a handbasket around here this morning when the snow started to fall."

She glanced around at the winter wonderland, understanding why he chose to live in this peaceful, beautiful slice of heaven. Even if living this far out of town probably came with complications.

"Don't sweat it. I haven't really had a lucky year." Or a lucky life for that matter, but a few months ago she'd decided not to wallow in self-pity anymore and it had worked. She laughed more. She forgot all about designer labels and getting married. She took one day at a time, did the task in front of her and didn't worry about tomorrow. And her life, even though it came with trouble, had become happier.

"Which is why you were driving back to your hometown?"

"No. I'm driving back to my hometown to see my sister. I'm interviewing for the temp job with you because of the bad year. My teaching position was cut. Rather than wait until I ran out of money and lost my apartment, I decided to go home. My sister owns a company and can give me a job the second I get to Newland, but I don't want to work in a bakery. I want to find a teaching job. And the few thousand dollars I'll make tutoring your son will give me a couple more weeks before I'll have to become a baker out of desperation." Especially since room and board came with the job.

He sniffed a confirming laugh that said he knew all about bad years, temp employment and desperation. But looking at his house, with multiple angles and levels of roofs, green shutters that accented the creamy yellow siding and gingerbread trim along the wraparound porch, she had to wonder if the guy really knew trouble. The house only needed gumdrops and candy canes to be ready for a storybook. People who lived in storybook houses didn't know trouble.

In her head, she snorted in derision. That's what everyone had believed about her family. But behind the walls of their perfect Cape Cod *home,* their father had ruled with an iron fist. Literally.

She shivered.

Clark's eyes widened. "I'm sorry. You're freezing. Let's go inside." He glanced back at her car. "Do you want me to grab your luggage?"

She smiled politely. "Let's see how the interview goes first."

He winced. "Right. Sorry." He pointed to the house and motioned for her to go before him. "Emily was so sure you'd be a good choice as Jack's homeschool facilitator that I took the liberty of checking the references on the résumé you emailed me. So we really are just down to the interview."

"That's good." She walked to the white porch steps and began climbing. The town she'd driven through at the bottom of the mountain had been decked out for Christmas. But this beautiful Victorian house, perfect for a dreamy holiday, didn't have as much as a string of lights along the porch roof.

"With my housekeeper sick for the past week, everything's been a little off-kilter. If I hadn't gone to the grocery store, I wouldn't even be able to offer you coffee." He stopped. "Shoot. I forgot the groceries. You go ahead inside. I'll get them."

She turned around with him. "I'll help."

"You're cold."

"And carrying groceries will warm me up."

She followed Clark to his SUV. He pulled out

two plastic bags with handles and she took them from him.

"Just go in the front door and follow it back down the hall to the kitchen."

She nodded, but by the time she got to the door in her slippery tennis shoes, Clark was right behind her.

"If you decide to take this job, you'll have to get yourself a pair of boots."

"I guess."

"And a coat. Winters can be brutal here."

The little girl who had been hanging on Clark's coat when she arrived stood in the front foyer. Wearing a pink hooded jacket and little white mittens, she looked both adorable and warm.

"This is Teagan."

The little girl's gaze dipped to the marble floor, so Althea stooped in front of her. "Hey, Teagan."

"Teagan, this is Ms. Johnson. She's the lady interviewing to be Jack's teacher."

Teagan continued to look at the floor.

"It was nice to meet you, Teagan." She rose. Sometimes it was best to give a child her space. Eventually, she'd warm up to her. Kids always did. With a quick smile at Teagan, she continued on to the kitchen.

Clark plopped his bags of groceries on the center island. Dark wood cabinets should have given the room a gloomy feel, but the cheerful white marble countertops and warm oak hardwood floors took care of that. So did the huge windows by the wooden table that provided a spectacular view of the mountains behind the house.

"Wow."

"Thank my wife for that view. She found this land, created the design for this house."

"She's got a real eye for things." She turned from the windows just as a boy of about twelve walked into the kitchen, the big black dog on his heels.

"Dad, did you get that ham I asked for?" When he saw Althea, he stopped dead in his tracks.

"Yes, I got the ham." He faced Althea. "Althea, that's my son, Jack." He turned to Jack. "Jack, this is Althea Johnson. As soon as I get these groceries put away I'm going to interview her to see if she can become your new teacher."

Taking a bag of cans to the pantry, Clark continued putting away the groceries. Big black dog by his side, Jack stood where he'd stopped, sizing her up.

Usually she wasn't afraid of a twelve-year-old boy, especially not one so handsome. Shaggy brown hair and big brown eyes like his dad's gave him an angelic choir-boy appearance. But he also had an odd expression on his face. Almost as if he were strategizing how to get her fired—and she hadn't even taken the job.

Clark came out of the pantry. "Okay, I'll make sandwiches. Jack, you finish with the groceries and then I can interview—" He stopped, faced Althea again. "I'm sorry. You'd said you hadn't eaten yet."

"I haven't."

"Okay, here's what we'll do. I'll make cocoa for the kids and then coffee for us before I make the sandwiches. Jack and Teagan can eat out here. We'll take our lunches into the den and we'll talk while we eat."

She wasn't the kind of person who got cozy so quickly with strangers. But when she'd turned over the new leaf about her life a few months back, she'd promised herself she'd stop being so cautious. Plus she was extremely hungry. The thought of a cup of coffee and a sandwich made her taste buds dance for joy.

Clark walked to the counter, opened a rollaway door and pulled out a coffeemaker. Feeling odd with nothing to do, she said, "I could put on the pot of coffee if you show me how."

On his way to the counter to get the groceries, Jack snorted a laugh. Clark faced her with a smile. "This is a single-serve coffeemaker. I can make two cups of cocoa for the kids and an individual cup of coffee for each of us."

"Oh." And didn't she feel stupid?

While the first cup of cocoa brewed, Clark whipped around the kitchen, gathering bread and ham and retrieving milk for the coffee from the fridge, along with condiments for their sandwiches. Teagan crawled up on one of the stools beside the center island where Clark opened the deli meat and a loaf of bread. The dog clip-clopped over to her, soundlessly parking herself beside Teagan's tall chair. Outside, the snow continued to fall. Big, beautiful white flakes on a huge, silent mountain.

Silent.

She glanced around. That's what bothered her.

It was as quiet in here as it was outside. Jack had put away the few things his father had directed him to, but he said nothing. Teagan sat on one of the tall chairs by the center island, just watching as Clark raced around, going between the coffeemaker and the refrigerator, gathering things for the sandwiches.

"Can I help with anything?"

"No. No. I'm fine. I'm accustomed to doing this."

Doing what? Getting lunch? Having quiet kids? Being a one-person whirlwind of activity? Because it was Tuesday, Althea suspected his wife was at work. So maybe when she was around everything was noisier?

With the ham, bread and condiments on the center island, Clark motioned for her to come over. "Fix yourself a sandwich while I make Teagan's cocoa."

She walked over, put bread on a paper plate and noticed Teagan watching her, her dark brown eyes cautious, curious. "I can make your sandwich first."

The little girl buried her face in the dirty pink bear she held. Though they'd been in the house ten minutes, she still wore her jacket with the hood on her head and her mittens on her hands.

Clark hustled over. She tugged on his shirtsleeve and he leaned down.

She whispered something in his ear.

He said, "Okay," and went back to the coffee/cocoa maker. "We don't have that flavor."

Her lips turned down in an adorable pout, as she slid her hood off. Her hair was as dark as her eyes. The pale pink coat she wore accented both. As pretty as a princess, she blinked at Althea.

"I can help you with your coat, if you want."

Teagan's gaze whipped to her dad. He walked over with a cup of cocoa. "I'll get her coat. You just finish making your sandwich."

Teagan tugged on his shirtsleeve again. He leaned down. She whispered in his ear.

Baffled, Althea stopped slathering mayonnaise on her bread. Not only did the little girl think it normal to talk only to her dad and only in a whisper, but also Clark was so accustomed to it, he automatically leaned down to listen.

"Sure. We have marshmallows."

She almost asked Clark about it. But she knew kids hated it when adults talked about them as if they weren't in the room. Any minute now she and Clark would go into the den for her interview. She could ask him then. Delicately of course.

"Jack, do you want to make your sandwich now, too, so that I can put all this stuff back in the fridge before we go into the den?"

Jack walked over, grabbed some bread and ham and fixed his sandwich without a word.

Althea's eyebrows rose. She'd taught middle school for six years. She knew twelve-year-olds. They were sassy, moody, and the boys were always hungry. They didn't wait for an invitation to make a sandwich.

What was going on here?

Clark handed Teagan her sandwich then he brought over her cocoa, complete with marshmallows, and started the first cup of coffee. He made his sandwich and the second cup of coffee then he put away the bread, ham and condiments before he faced the kids.

"Althea and I will be in the den. If you need me, just come back and get me."

Teagan blinked. Jack nodded.

She followed Clark down a long hall off the front foyer to the den. He motioned for her to take the empty chair in front of the desk then sat on the tall-back chair behind it.

"I think we should just get right to the point."

She nodded, knowing what was coming. With a housekeeper in the hospital with pneumonia and a wife who obviously worked, this job had morphed into babysitter/teacher. She might even have to cook. Or clean up. It was not going to be the piece-of-cake, easy-money job she'd expected. Not that she was above helping out. Plus, truth be told, taking this position was about more than money. Spending four weeks close to her sister, but not really in Maryland was a stall tactic. She longed to see her sister. But she was afraid to see her dad. So finding employment close enough that Missy could drive up and visit her here in Pennsylvania might have been too good to be true.

That was usually how her life worked. Everything she thought was "perfect" ended up being a scam.

She smiled slightly. "Sure. Let's just get right to the point."

"My wife was killed in an automobile accident three years ago."

Her mouth dropped a bit. That wasn't at all what she'd been expecting. From the casual way he'd mentioned her when she complimented the view, she never would have guessed his wife had died. She'd even suspected the poor woman was at work.

"Jack did okay until this fall. Now suddenly he's failing all his classes. He's done so poorly that his former teacher quit. I need you to pack four months of learning into one month."

"That's quite a job."

"He's been over the material once already. Technically only the December material will be new." He leaned back in his chair. "He's not a stupid kid. In fact, he's very bright. I'm sure he's retained some of what he heard. This is more about getting him focused again and making him see that if he decides to slack off, there are consequences."

"Are you sure this isn't about him grieving for his mom?"

Clark sighed. "She died three years ago. He had two therapy sessions. One right after. One about a year ago. He has the techniques and tools to cope."

"But he's in a new life phase. And I'm not a therapist—"

"If you think he needs to begin seeing his therapist again, back he'll go. But I think this is more about him getting soft than anything to do with his mom. Twelve is a normal rebellion stage." He winced. "I know that because I went through one myself."

When she pictured rebellion, she didn't picture silence. She envisioned anger. Pouting, sure. But not the control and quiet she'd seen in that kitchen.

Still, he'd said if she believed his son needed to talk to someone he would get him help. She couldn't argue that.

"So, what makes you want a temporary job?"

"As I said, I lost my job and I'm on my way to live with my sister in Maryland. I want the extra cash to give me more time to look for a teaching job."

He nodded as if remembering their conversation outside.

"Plus, she has triplets and a new husband I haven't yet met."

He frowned. "You haven't met your sister's family?"

She shrugged that off easily. She could answer this without giving away any of her secrets. "California's a long way from here. I didn't have the money to just pop home and I also couldn't take the time off work."

Accepting that, he shifted on his chair, getting more comfortable, a sign that the interview was going well from his perspective.

"Since Jack's original homeschooling program failed, I found three excellent replacement options you can use to catch him up on this semester, but there are also some incredible subject-specific websites you can use to reinforce the material."

"Sounds like you've done your homework."

"Being a single parent is something like a full-time job."

She inclined her head. She understood what was going on. He could easily handle the concrete and the obvious. Parental duties and tasks, things he could see. Insubstantial, delicate things like talking weren't as easily handled as getting groceries, finding homeschool programs or making lunch. He might be ignoring warning signs because he didn't know to look for them.

He smiled. "Do you have any questions for me?"

"Yes. I'd like to know about Teagan."

"Do you mean what will Teagan do while you teach Jack?" He tossed a pencil to his desk. "I was hoping she could color in the room you and Jack use for your class work."

"Actually, I'm more concerned about the way she only talks to you and then only in a whisper."

He laughed. "She's three-and-a-half. She's just shy."

Three-and-a-half? And her mom had died three years ago? The poor thing had been only six months old when her mom died. Technically, she didn't know her own mother. And he thought she didn't talk because she was shy?

"Really? You think she's just shy?"

"Yes. She's fine."

Althea took a bite of her sandwich to stop herself from saying something she might regret. Either this guy was in complete denial about his kids or he was right.

If he was right, if Jack was in the throes of a

normal twelve-year-old rebellion and Teagan was just shy, everything would work itself out. If he wasn't—

Well, if he wasn't, these kids were suffering. They might not be huddled in a closet, desperately trying to block out the sounds of their dad beating their mom the way she and her older sister Missy had been, but they were suffering. And if their dad didn't understand, there was no one to help them.

She knew she might be reading too much into this situation, but after her own miserable childhood, when every teacher, every neighbor, and even her grandmother missed the signs that she, her sister and her mom were in trouble, she couldn't just walk away.

"I'll take the job."

He sat up. "Really?"

The disbelief in his voice made her laugh. "You were afraid that when I'd realized I may also have to become your temporary housekeeper/babysitter this week, I'd refuse."

"I wasn't going to ask you to do the housekeeping, but if you could at least tidy up after meals it would be a big help."

Drat. Her and her big mouth.

"I have some projects at work that I should be attending to. If you could start today, I could get an afternoon of research in. I'll work from here, of course, so you and the kids will have today to get accustomed to each other. But I really do need to catch up. I missed all of last week."

His hopeful voice made her shake her head. What the heck? She wasn't doing anything else. And the sooner she sat down with these kids and tried to figure everything out, the better.

"As long as I don't have to cook."

"You can't cook?"

"No reason to cook when I lived alone."

"I'll get takeout."

She glanced across the desk at him with a smile to confirm their deal, but he rose and extended his hand to shake hers. She stood up. When she took his hand, a bolt of electricity crackled up her arm. Their eyes met and from the quick glimmer in his, she knew he'd felt it as clearly as she had.

Her gaze fell from his handsome face to his sweater-covered chest to his snug blue jeans and the crackle of electricity sparked again.

She stifled the urge to yank her hand away. It

was one thing to take a job as a live-in employee, knowing *she* was attracted to her employer. She'd always been able to ignore her hormones.

But knowing he was attracted to her, too—

Weren't they tempting fate?

CHAPTER TWO

CLARK WALKED AROUND the desk. "Let's get your things from your car and I'll give you the grand tour of the house."

He motioned for her to precede him out of the den. She headed for the door and he followed, his gaze automatically dipping to her butt.

With a wince, he forced his eyes back up again. What was he doing? Yes, Althea was pretty with her sunny yellow hair and big blue eyes, and, yes, he'd felt that zap of electricity when they shook hands, but she was now his employee.

Even if she wasn't, he wasn't interested. He could have cited the usual reasons. Losing his wife so suddenly had been a shock. But discovering she'd been having an affair and that her lover was someone he'd considered a friend—that had about killed him.

The echo of the pain of the first few months after her accident still lingered. Memories of consoling Jack, the chaos of caring for a six-month-old baby alone, the cool, empty feeling of his bed, all rose up inside him every time he thought about moving on. But none of those were as bad as the ache. The solid ball of grief that weighed him down, sat in his belly like lead, even as it competed with the hurt and humiliation of discovering she'd been having an affair.

The woman he'd believed would love him forever, the woman who'd borne his children, had betrayed him.

That kind of humiliation left more than a mark. It changed a man's perspective. Caused him to make vows—and keep them.

He would never be vulnerable again.

Never.

That's why he wasn't worried about his attraction to Jack's new teacher. He was too smart to be tempted to even consider trusting someone again.

Plus, her résumé might say she was twenty-eight but she looked twenty-two. He'd already been made the town laughingstock. He didn't need to add chasing after a woman who looked too young for him.

When he and Althea reached the front door, he

opened it for her. She looked back at him with a smile. "Thanks."

His heart tumbled in his chest. Had he thought her pretty? He'd been wrong. When she smiled she was breathtaking.

But he wasn't interested. "You're welcome."

They stepped out onto the snow-covered porch and he grimaced. "I should have gotten you a coat."

She glanced at him skeptically. "You have one that would fit?"

He wanted to drown in her big blue eyes and for a smart man that didn't make sense. He'd already set his mind not to trust again and that precluded falling in love, or even indulging an attraction. But how could he stop an attraction? The bubbly feeling that rose when she looked at him was natural, spontaneous.

And annoying. He hated being out of control.

"No, but even a too big coat would be better than an insubstantial hoodie."

She laughed.

The sound skipped along his nerve endings, filling him with pleasure. Damn it! Why was this happening?

She jogged down the steps. "Can't argue that. But since we're out here already, let's just grab my suitcases and do the tour so you can get to work and I can spend some time with Jack."

He couldn't argue that. With his hormones going haywire, the less time they spent together, the better.

Her things turned out to be two suitcases, an overnight bag and a laptop. He carried the two suitcases. She carried the rest. He led her down the hall to the kitchen again, then to the suite of rooms behind it.

"Mrs. Alwine stays here when I travel. But while you're here, the suite is all yours."

She made a slow turn, taking in the big dresser and mirrored vanity, as well as the aqua-and-brown comforter and pillows that matched the aqua-and-brown print curtains.

She faced him with a frown. "So in other words, if you travel while I'm here, I'm in charge of the kids overnight."

Heat crawled up his neck. He hadn't even considered that might be presumptuous, then realized he'd done the same thing to Mrs. Alwine. The heat intensified. If there was one thing he prided himself on it was doing his fair share. Not leaving the kids to their own devices. But it seemed in being so careful of the kids, he'd been a little heavy handed with his employees.

"I guess that depends on when Mrs. Alwine comes back."

She laughed and slid out of her jacket. A rust-colored T-shirt outlined perfect breasts and a small waist. With a quick shake of her head, her sunny yellow hair swirled around her and fell in place on her shoulders.

His mouth watered, and he cursed inside his head. With her hoodie gone, she didn't look twenty-two anymore. She looked all twenty-eight of the years he'd seen on her résumé. But instead of that making her less desirable, it made her more desirable. She was right in his age range—not too young for him as she'd looked in the hoodie.

He pivoted to face the door. That kind of thinking wouldn't do either one of them any good. He needed her help. She needed some money. For both of them to get what they wanted—what they needed—they had to keep this relationship strictly platonic.

"I'll round up the kids and you can do what you want this afternoon. Maybe let Jack have a hand in choosing the new homeschooling program."

She nodded, but he didn't hang around. He bounded out of the room, found the kids, and got them set up in the den.

When everyone was settled around the big desk, Jack behind the computer, Althea on the chair beside him, and Teagan on the opposite side with her coloring book, he said, "Okay. Now I'm going upstairs to my office to work."

He closed the den door behind him with a giant sigh of relief. But Althea faced his two quiet children with a sigh of confusion.

Seeing the look of exasperation on Jack's face, she clicked off the computer monitor. "I just got here. You just met me." She smiled at Jack, then Teagan. "I don't think we should work this afternoon."

Jack said, "All right!" But Teagan jumped off her chair, scampered over to Jack and frantically tugged on his shirtsleeve.

He leaned down, rolled his eyes, then caught Althea's gaze. "She still wants to color."

"Oh, sweetie! You can color, if that's fun for

you. I'm just saying that neither your brother nor I was prepared to work today so I don't think we should."

Teagan didn't really pay attention to what Althea said. From the second the words, "You can color," came out of her mouth, the little girl raced back to her chair and put her attention on a fat coloring book and a box of brightly colored crayons.

The temptation was strong to ask Jack if she was always like this. Then she remembered Missy. She remembered how as older sister Missy had ended up assuming responsibilities that shouldn't have been hers, and she pulled back her question.

For all she knew, having to speak for his three-year-old sister could be part of the reason Jack was unhappy.

"So, do you want to play Yahtzee or Uno or something?"

Jack laughed. "Really?"

"Well, we can't just sit here and do nothing. Plus you can learn a lot from how somebody plays a game."

He slouched down on his seat with a huff and

folded his arms across his chest. "You're going to analyze me."

"No, I'm going to get to know you. And if you're smart you'll also use the time to get to know me."

He sniffed a laugh. "Right." He sat up. "But I'd rather play video games."

She winced. "I'm not very good."

"Then I guess we'll see if you have a temper."

This time she laughed. "You're pretty smart for a twelve-year-old."

"Yeah. That's why I'm failing all my classes."

It would have been the perfect opportunity to get into a discussion about his classes and what he thought might have caused his bad semester, but he gave the video game instructions so quickly she didn't have time to ask. He handed her a controller and pointed at the spot beside him on the sofa. Thrust into a game she'd never seen before, she needed all her concentration just to work the controller.

In between rounds, she glanced at Teagan who quietly colored in her fat book. After an hour or so of the game, Jack said, "Hey, Chai Tea."

Teagan looked over.

"Isn't it about time for your nap?"

She slid off her chair just as the den door opened and Clark stepped inside. He stooped down and opened his arms. "I see somebody's ready for a nap."

He scooped up the little girl, and, as he rose, he saw the video game. "I thought you'd be working."

"Today is our first day together," Althea said, then added a, "Drat" when Jack killed two of her soldiers. "Anyway, we're using this time to get to know each other."

Without taking his eyes off the screen, Jack said, "We're bonding."

"Just don't bond too long. I want your grades up so you don't fall behind a semester."

He left the room and Jack tossed his controller to the sofa. "Let's go."

Baffled, she turned, her gaze following him as he walked to the desk. "Go?"

"To work. You heard him. He wants my grades up."

She rose from the sofa. "Yes. But he didn't seem to be angry that we were getting to know each other."

"You should have spent some time bonding with my dad instead of me. Then you'd know that was his angry voice."

"*That* was his angry voice?"

"Yep."

They went to the computer and checked out the potential programs Clark had chosen for his son. Jack participated as they scrolled through each one, but his responses were lackluster. She tried to revive some of the enthusiasm he'd shown while playing video games, and though he would smile, his heart clearly wasn't in his studies.

The den door opened again. Clark poked his head inside. "I ordered pizza. It should be here in a half hour or so. Jack, I'm sure Althea would appreciate the chance to clean up before we eat. So why don't you turn everything off so she can go?"

"What time is it?"

"Six."

"Six!" It had been noon when she'd arrived, probably after one before they finished the interview and got her set up in her room. That could have made it two when she and the kids got settled in the den. Maybe three before Teagan left for her nap. That meant she and Jack had spent three hours looking at programs. She supposed that wasn't too far-fetched.

"Where's Teagan?"

"After her nap, she stayed in the office with me."

"Oh. Okay." She smiled at Jack. "You and I certainly were immersed in our work."

He smiled. But he didn't say anything. She glanced at Clark then back at Jack.

He wasn't afraid of his father. *That* she recognized from her own life. She knew what a frightened child looked like. But he was terribly unhappy.

She followed Clark to the kitchen, ducked into her suite behind it to wash her hands, then joined Clark and Teagan at the table. While Jack found paper plates and napkins, Clark opened the big pizza box. The scent of tomato sauce and pepperoni invaded the air, making Althea's stomach growl.

"I guess this is what two days of going without food will do to you."

Clark gaped at her. "You really did go without food?"

"I wanted to get here. I'd already been on the road three days. After I talked to Emily, I just wanted to keep moving so I could get here and get started."

"I can understand that." He glanced back at Jack. "Hurry up, buddy, or the pizza will be cold."

At the easy way the term of endearment slipped from Clark's lips, Althea frowned. He clearly loved his son. And with Teagan sitting on his lap while he cut her pizza into tiny pieces, it was also obvious that he loved his daughter. He was simply too much of an organizer. Someone who wanted everything to run like a well-oiled machine. Because everything was "working" he didn't see anything wrong.

But there was plenty wrong. She could see it in Jack's eyes.

They ate their pizza with Clark carrying on a steady stream of chitchat. When he announced he would be getting Teagan ready for bed, she asked if she could follow along.

His face scrunched in confusion. "Why?"

"With the housekeeper gone, it's just good for me to know all the routines."

He shrugged. "Sure. Great."

She trailed behind him as he carried the little girl up the steps. They found her bedclothes first, then Teagan had a quick bath. She slipped into her princess nightgown and crawled under the covers.

Althea leaned against the doorjamb as Clark retrieved a well-worn storybook from the drawer in the white bedside table that matched the white frame of her canopy bed.

He read her a story about a bunny that had gotten lost in the woods. While most children's eyes would droop as the story lulled them to sleep, Teagan's eyes widened.

Althea frowned. Why read her a story that seemed to upset her?

But in the end the daddy rabbit found the lost bunny. He fed her soup, tucked her into bed and kissed her forehead, telling her he'd never let anything happen to her. She could always depend on him.

Happy ending.

Clark rose, tucked Teagan into bed, kissed her forehead and said, "I'll never let anything happen to you." He kissed her forehead again. "You can always depend on me."

Teagan smiled. Her eyelids finally lowered. She snuggled into her pillow.

Warmth filled Althea's soul. Using a story he had just told his daughter he'd always be there for her. A pretty smart move for a guy who obviously didn't know how to say the words himself.

Clark motioned to the door. Althea turned and walked out into the hall with him on her heels, and the glow in her warming every part of her body. This was definitely a family worth saving.

But how?

The next morning when Althea stumbled into the kitchen, she found the quiet Beaumonts all seated on the tall stools around the center island.

"Good morning."

Clark glanced up from his computer screen. "Good morning."

Today he wore dark trousers, white shirt and blue tie. His hair neatly combed and his brown eyes bright with enthusiasm, he was clearly happy to be getting back to his normal routine.

Her attraction sparked to life again, but, as always with anything to do with her hormones, she ignored it. As she prepared a single cup of coffee using the directions on the side of the coffeemaker, she nodded at his laptop. "Working already?"

"Reading the *Wall Street Journal* online."

Now why in the name of all that was holy had that sounded sexy? "Ah."

She ambled to the center island. Clark pointed at a plate of French toast. "Breakfast?"

"Yeah. As soon as I have at least one cup of coffee."

He rose and grabbed the black suit coat from the back of his stool. "If everything's under control here, I'm going to go into the office right now. Even with email and fax machines, we couldn't get everything done we needed to get done last week while I was home with the kids. And we're hopelessly behind in preparing some important government bids."

He shrugged into the charcoal-gray overcoat that had been flung across the unused table by the French doors.

"You never did tell me what you do for a living."

"I own an engineering firm."

"Oh." The way he said that sounded sexy, too,

confusing her. She wasn't the kind of woman to fall for the executive type. She had been a sucker for beach bums. Which was why she kept getting her heart broken and her bank account depleted and why she'd stopped dating.

He motioned for her to walk him to the front door. When they were out of earshot of the kitchen he said, "My wife was the brains of the operation. She was actually the engineer. I'm just a lowly liberal arts major who took business courses at university after we realized Carol wanted to start her own firm, and she'd need me to run it. When she died, I had to hire two people to replace her."

The casual, very calm way he talked about his deceased wife baffled her. Until she remembered that was sort of how Clark talked about everything. Casually. Calmly. With very little emotion.

"I also had to learn as much about the work as I possibly could so that I could speak intelligently to clients."

"So you've had a long, difficult three years."

Reaching for the doorknob, he frowned. "I would think that would go without saying."

Yeah. She supposed he was right.

"Anyway, I'll be back around six. All of my contact numbers are on a sheet in the kitchen. As you probably noticed yesterday, Teagan is fine coloring or playing by herself. Do whatever you would normally do with Jack's lessons, etc. And then spend the rest of the day however you want."

"You'll bring dinner?"

He chuckled. "Yes."

With a quick yank on the front door, he opened it and left.

She took her time returning to the kitchen. He wasn't a bad guy. Actually, he seemed like a really nice guy—a *gorgeous* nice guy to whom she was unexpectedly attracted. But he was an executive who'd handled his wife's death with the cool efficiency he probably spent on the company's tax return. He had to use a storybook to show his daughter she could depend on him.

It wasn't his fault that his kids were quiet, sad. Maybe even slightly lost. He handled things the way he knew how.

But his kids *were* quiet and sad, and slightly lost, and she ached for them.

In the kitchen, she glanced at Jack who wore jeans and a T-shirt then Teagan who wore little blue jeans with pink flowers embroidered on the pockets with a matching pink T-shirt. Her long dark hair had been combed, even though she didn't have a clip or band to keep it out of her face.

She ambled to the center island, filled a plate with two slices of French toast and sat on the stool beside Teagan.

"Are you ready to color today?"

The little girl yanked on Jack's sleeve. He bent down and she whispered in his ear.

Jack sighed. "She said yes."

Althea poured syrup on her toast, her heart aching for Jack again. The kid was twelve, isolated on a mountaintop—a beautiful mountaintop to be sure, but a lonely one. And a boy who should be in the ignoring-his-siblings stage had to speak for his baby sister.

He needed some fun.

And not just video games. Something unexpected.

"We're going on a field trip this morning."

Jack gaped at her. "Field trip?"

"Yeah. I need a coat and boots."

Teagan blinked at her. Jack frowned. "You don't have a coat?"

"I lived in Southern California for the past ten years. The heaviest thing I have is a hoodie."

Jack just stared at her.

"Come on. You're old enough to know the geography of this country. We have all different kinds of weather."

"I suppose. I just don't want my dad to be mad."

"He's the one who told me to get boots."

She turned him toward the door. "Go get your coat and your sister's coat. I swear we'll have fun."

CHAPTER THREE

JACK REMINDED ALTHEA that Teagan was too small to ride in a car without a safety seat, so they grabbed the extra one from the garage and installed it in her little red car.

The whole time they worked, Althea kept glancing back at Teagan, hoping for her to speak. Clearly excited at the prospect of getting out of the house, the little girl jumped from foot to foot. Her eyes glowed. Her smile could light the garage. But she never said a word.

As they rode down the hill, Jack chatted happily, filling her chest with the light airy feeling that comes from pleasing another person. She'd figured out he needed to get out of the house, she just hadn't realized how badly. It was a stroke of luck that she needed a coat and boots.

She parked in front of one of the meters, fed it enough to give them an hour for shopping and turned the kids in the direction of the town's general store.

In a shop stocked for winter in the mountains, she immediately found a coat and boots. The light blue jacket, black mittens and black boots she tried on not only fit, they were cute. But because she found them so quickly, their trip into town was ending too soon.

So, wearing her new coat and boots, she herded the kids across the street, telling them she wanted to see more of the town. About halfway down, she got her second lucky break of the morning: a Santa Shop.

There was nothing like seeing decorations, talking about gifts and sharing secret gift wishes to perk up children.

"Why don't we take a peek inside?"

Jack's face scrunched in confusion. "You want to go into a Santa Shop?"

"Yes."

"Why?"

"Why not?"

"Because we don't decorate until Christmas Eve?"

She took Teagan's hand. "Well, maybe we should

change that this year and do some decorating beforehand?"

Teagan blinked up at her silently. It wasn't much, but she suspected eye contact was a big step for Teagan.

Jack shook his head. "If Dad hates us decorating early, I'm telling him it was all your idea."

"Good. Fine. Because it is my idea. And if he loves it I'll get all the credit."

When they reached the shop door, Jack held it open like a perfect gentleman. The scents of cinnamon, apples and bayberry wafted out to them. Old-fashioned wooden tables held rows of toy soldiers. Model trains chugged in circles around miniature towns. Ceramic villages took up another two rows. Evergreen wreaths hung on the back walls beside bundles of tinsel.

"I can't afford much," she told the kids, "but we're four weeks away from Christmas. The least we should get today is a wreath for the door. Then we'll come back every week and get something new."

Jack faced her. "You want *us* to pick out the wreath?"

"Sure. It's for your house. Your Christmas."

He stood in front of her, looking totally puzzled.

"I thought you said you decorated on Christmas Eve?"

"We do. But we only put up a tree. Dad says it's enough."

"Well, sure it's enough," she agreed, not wanting to undermine his dad or make him look bad. "But starting today and doing a little something every week to the house, a little something to remind us that in a few weeks we'll get presents and drink hot cocoa by the fire and eat peppermint sticks—well, that'll just make everything extra special."

Jack laughed lightly. "I think you're expecting a lot from a wreath."

Holding Teagan's hand, she headed for the wreaths. "You'll see. Maybe not this week but next week it will all start to sink in and then we'll have Christmas spirit all over the place."

Following a few feet behind her, Jack laughed.

Althea's spirits soared. Teagan might not be talking but she was happy. And Jack was laughing. Once they got the wreath, they could go home and start his lessons.

* * *

Around eleven o'clock, Clark began to get antsy. He'd been so focused on how much work he'd missed because of Mrs. Alwine that he hadn't thought through leaving the kids that morning.

Technically, Althea wasn't a total stranger. She was a friend of a friend. That was how she'd gotten wind of the job and why he'd agreed to interview her. Yes, he'd checked her references. But he didn't *know* her. And he'd left his kids with her.

He fished his cell phone out of his jacket pocket and hit the speed dial number for his home phone. It rang the usual four times before it went to voice mail.

He sucked in a breath. She could be in the bathroom. Or she might have turned off the ringer of the phone in the den for Jack's studying.

Or she could have kidnapped his kids.

He groaned internally, telling himself not to think like that, and rummaged around on his desk for the sheet of paper with her cell phone number on it.

When he finally found it, he punched in the digits and waited through five rings before it, too, went to voice mail.

He tossed his cell phone to the desk, telling himself not to be paranoid. But his situation was unusual. There was a reason he lived on a secluded mountaintop. A reason he hid his kids. Even discounting the possibility that someone might kidnap them because he was a wealthy man who could pay a ransom, lots of people were curious about Teagan.

He cursed, shot off his chair and grabbed his top coat. Walking through his assistant's office, he said, "I'm going home," and strode out to his SUV.

Even wanting to get to his house as quickly as possible, he made a loop around town and headed up the mountain. As his SUV rolled to a stop in front of the garage, his chest tightened. Althea's car was gone.

Frantic, he flew up the porch steps and into the foyer, calling the kids' names. No answer. Nothing but the eerie echo of his own words came back to him. Crazy clip-clopped into the foyer, nudging her nose against Clark's hand for a pat on the top of her head.

Clark stooped to pet the nuzzling dog, but his mind jumped back to the day he'd gotten the call about his wife. He'd come home from a business trip to a cold, empty house and had no idea where his kids were, let alone his wife. Then the phone had rung and he'd gotten the news that his wife was dead and his kids were with her parents.

He broke out in a cold sweat.

Cold, empty houses were never good news.

And with a guy in town who might suspect he was Teagan's father, a guy crazy enough to throw himself over Clark's wife's casket and wail—not worried about gossip or consequences—Clark couldn't take any chances Brice Matthews would see Teagan.

Even if the kids were safe with Althea, that didn't mean they were safe from Brice.

He pulled out his cell phone and dialed 9-1-1.

Though they purchased a wreath and secured it in her trunk, Althea took the kids around town to visit a few more shops and scope out potential decorations they'd buy in the following weeks. Now that she'd talked Jack into decorating the house for Christmas, she wanted to see her options.

They had just walked out of the last shop,

laughing as they ate ice cream, even though it was freezing out, when two policemen rushed them.

One policeman grabbed Jack and Teagan. The other backed her into the shop wall.

"Are you Althea Johnson?"

"Yes?"

Teagan began to cry. Jack tried to squirm out of the officer's hold. "Let go of me."

"And these children are Jack and Teagan Beaumont?"

"Yes."

"We have a report that you took these kids from their home."

"I'm their babysitter. We came to town to look for a coat and boots for me." She motioned to her brand-new blue jacket and still shiny black boots. "Call their dad. He'll tell you I'm their babysitter."

"He's the one who filed the report."

Clark's SUV slid to a stop in front of the sidewalk. He bounded out and raced over, grabbing Teagan from the officer and then pulling Jack under his arm protectively. "Are you guys okay?"

Jack looked at him as if he were crazy. "We were fine until you called the police on us."

Teagan buried her face in her father's neck. Clark's expression hardened. "Teagan is not fine."

"She was," Jack insisted. "She was laughing."

Standing on tiptoes to see over the policeman's shoulder, Althea shouted, "She was. We were having fun."

"You were supposed to be home!"

"We were on our way home to start Jack's lessons. We had plenty of time. We just shifted our schedule." She pointed at her jacket. "I needed a coat. And boots." She held up her foot, displaying one of her new boots. "Remember?"

The policeman holding her back faced Clark. "So what's going on here?"

"We were just shopping!" Jack spat. "But I get it! He doesn't ever want us doing anything that might even remotely be fun." He shrugged out from beneath his dad's hold and headed for the SUV. "Take us home. Put us back in jail."

Saddened for Jack, Althea swallowed, glanced at Clark, then pressed her lips together.

A mixture of horror and confusion played across

Clark's face. As if finally putting it all together in his head, he stepped back. "Oh, my God."

He looked from Jack who stood beside his SUV to Teagan in his arms to Althea still backed up against the shop wall, and scrubbed his hand across his mouth. "Oh, my God. I'm so sorry."

The policeman released Althea. "So everything's good?"

Althea forced a smile. She didn't know whether to be angry with herself for not letting Clark know she was taking the kids shopping, annoyed with him for being so damned paranoid, or to feel sorry for him.

In the end, she decided to feel sorry for him. He'd lost his wife. He didn't want to lose his kids, too. She got it. "Everything's fine. Really. Let me get them home."

The policeman looked to Clark for confirmation. He nodded. "I'm sorry. I panicked." He nearly said, "Ever since my wife's death I've been panicky," but he knew that would only make him look like an idiot. God knew it made him *feel* like an idiot. So he said nothing.

The two policemen walked back to their car.

Althea ambled over, looking warm and snuggly in her new blue coat and black mittens. "Are you sure you're okay?"

He put his head back, closed his eyes. He'd just had her nabbed by the cops and she was asking him if he was okay? "I should be asking you that. I'm so sorry." He opened his eyes and forced himself to look at her. "You have the right to use whatever schedule you want." He sucked in a breath. "But I don't like the kids going into town without me. I wish you had called me before you left the house."

"You're right. I should have called you." She pressed her hand to her chest. "That's my mistake. I never thought to call. But I should have."

She put her hand on his arm consolingly. "Let's go home."

He couldn't believe she wanted to go with him. Were he in her shoes, he'd probably quit. But when he pulled his SUV off Main Street and onto the mountain road, she was right behind him. When he drove onto his lane, her little red car was in his rearview mirror. When he got out, she got out.

They walked into the echoing foyer with Teagan asleep on his arm. A dull sound rang in his ears, making his head pound. He'd never been so mortified.

Or so confused. Jack thought they lived in a jail? Teagan had laughed with an outsider?

Althea said, "Why don't you put her on her bed and I'll make us all some cocoa."

Jack sniffed with disdain. "I don't want any cocoa."

All the control he thought he had slipped through his fingers like melted snow. "Good. You can go into the den and take a look at today's lesson."

"Whatever."

He watched Jack stalk away and knew he'd handled that badly, but his head hurt and his thoughts swam like fish in a bowl. How had he gotten to this place?

He slid his gaze to Althea. "I don't need any cocoa."

"Bourbon then?"

A surprised laugh escaped. "Actually, bourbon sounds really good right now. But I'll be fine. You go work with Jack."

She shook her head. "Jack needs a minute.

Forcing him to set things up on the computer by himself will be a good way to occupy him and give him some space."

He took Teagan to her room and lingered over removing her coat and boots. There wasn't any part of him that wanted to confide in anyone, let alone Jack's teacher—a woman he was actually attracted to. But, more than that, he was mortified that he'd panicked. And not just panicked. He'd panicked publicly. He'd called the police when his kids were happily strolling down Main Street.

Of course, he hadn't known that.

Still, a sensible man would have at least looked in the obvious places—

But a man who'd been blindsided by his wife's death and double blindsided by her infidelity jumped to all kinds of conclusions.

When he couldn't delay any longer, he walked downstairs. Hoping Althea had gone to the den to be with Jack, he turned right, into the living room, and there she stood in front of the discreet bar housed in a black built-in beside a huge window. She held a short glass with two fingers of bourbon.

She handed it to him. "Is neat good?"

He smiled. "I don't sully whiskey with frozen water."

She laughed. "Have a seat."

He lowered himself to the gray sofa. "You're going to quit, aren't you?"

She sat on one of the two white club chairs across from him. A glass-and-chrome coffee table sat on the gray, white and black printed rug that connected the small conversation group in the big living room.

"I'm not going to quit."

"I sent the police after you."

"You were afraid."

He downed his drink, savoring the soothing warmth as it ran down his throat. He rose to get another. "Right."

"I saw the look on your face. You were terrified."

He grabbed the bourbon bottle and poured.

"You'd thought I'd taken your kids. There has to be a reason you were so suspicious."

"I was angry with myself for leaving the kids with someone I really didn't know."

"Maybe. But something pushed you to the point that you panicked rather than check things out."

He sighed. This time he sipped the whiskey. There was no way in hell he'd recount his private failures to a stranger. A stranger he'd wronged no less.

"All right. You don't want to talk. I get it. But I also see your kids are in trouble emotionally and so are you."

He snorted in disgust. "Are you saying we all need therapy?"

"I'm saying you need to give yourself a break and need to give your kids a break. You're over-organized. Your kids seem to feel they need to be super quiet to please you."

Heat of shame filled him. The day before, he'd noticed that he'd been taking advantage of Mrs. Alwine. Was it such a big stretch to consider that he'd forced his kids to overbehave?

He ambled back to his seat. She rose from hers. "I can understand that you don't want the help of a stranger. I'm also not a therapist. But I have spent six years with kids Jack's age. I know they sass. I know they experiment with cursing. I know they sulk and whine and roll their eyes and in general make the lives of adults miserable. And Jack does a few of those things, but not often. He's too concerned with pleasing you." She sucked in a breath. "You have an opportunity here. It's four weeks before Christmas. Four weeks when you can decorate together, tell him stories about Christmases past with his mom. Watch old Christmas movies. Make snowmen. Sled ride."

He raised his gaze to meet hers.

"The choice is yours. Use Christmas to turn your family into a family again. Or let this go on. Pretend Teagan's not talking is shyness. Pretend Jack's simmering silence is part of being a twelve-year-old. And six years from now when Jack leaves home without a word of why, and with no intention of ever coming back, you'll have no one to blame but yourself."

Jack's angry comment about living in prison rumbled through his brain. He was failing as a father and though he was loathe to talk about any of this, he'd be a fool if he didn't realize he was drowning.

He blew his breath out, rubbed his hand across his mouth and finally decided he had no choice.

He didn't want his kids to hate him or to be unhappy. But he also didn't want them going into town, and if the way to keep them home was to tell their current babysitter the whole story then maybe that's what he had to do.

"The day my wife died, I came home from work to find the house empty and cold."

"So when you came here today and found we'd gone, the empty house scared you?"

"Not as much as having the kids go to town." He scrubbed his hands across his mouth again. He hated this. Hated his misery. His humiliation. But he did not want his kids in town. "My wife had been having an affair. Apparently for at least a year. Brice Matthews, one of our employees, showed up at the funeral overcome with grief and sobbed over her coffin. He called me every name in the book for not letting her go—not giving her a divorce—when she'd never asked for a divorce."

"Oh, my God." Clearly shocked, she sat again. "I'm so sorry."

"That's why I don't want the kids in town."

"Because of gossip?" She shook her head. "It's

been three years. Trust me. You can stop worrying. People aren't that interested in anybody's life."

"Everybody's interested in Teagan's."

Her eyes narrowed. "Teagan's? Jack's the one old enough to understand—" Then her mouth dropped open. "Oh, God. Teagan was only a few months old when your wife died and your wife had been having an affair."

"For a year before she died."

"You think people wonder if she's yours?"

"I don't think. I *know* lots wonder whether or not she's really mine."

"They've told you this?"

"No. But a few days after Carol's death, people started looking at Teagan oddly. If I'd go to the grocery store with her in a carrier, everybody peeked in to see her. Some people were more obvious than others. It took me a while, but I realized everybody thought she was Brice's child and they were looking at her to see if there was a resemblance."

"That's awful." She shook her head again, as if marveling at the stupidity of some people. "I'm sorry."

"That's the second time you've said that." He

sniffed a laugh. "And I appreciate the sentiment. But you certainly weren't at fault."

"I know. But on behalf of crappy, unfair things that happen everywhere, I feel somebody has to say they're sorry."

He laughed again. His chest loosened. The knot in his stomach unwound.

Their gazes met and he smiled. "Thanks."

"On behalf of crappy things everywhere, you're welcome."

"No. I meant thanks for listening." He rubbed his hand along the back of his neck. "You're the first person I've told this story to." And he didn't feel god-awful. He felt calm, almost normal. "Anyway, that's why I don't want the kids to go into town. I don't want Teagan subjected to scrutiny or Jack to hear things about his mom he's too young to understand."

"Got it." She rose, smiled briefly. "Jack's probably got the computer up and running by now."

With that she left the room, and he flopped back on the sleek gray sofa, looking at the gorgeously appointed living room in the house so well designed "perfect" was too small of a term to use to describe it. In the end, the "perfect" house had meant nothing. Absolutely nothing.

His wife had cheated. Her affair had started before Teagan was conceived. And if Brice Matthews ever figured that out, he might lose Teagan long before he lost Jack.

He sipped his bourbon and closed his eyes. His life was a mess and though he appreciated Althea's suggestion about decorating, he didn't think decorating for Christmas was going to change that.

But at least he knew Althea would keep the kids home now.

CHAPTER FOUR

"I THINK I have a problem."

Even though she'd closed the den door, Althea walked down the hall, away from the room, so the kids couldn't hear her as she talked with her sister, Missy.

After her discussion with Clark, she'd tried to imagine what it would be like to lose a spouse, a wife he'd obviously believed loved him, discover she'd been unfaithful, and have poor, innocent Teagan's parentage called into question by the town gossips. The humiliation would be off the charts. But couple that with grief? She couldn't fathom the pain of that.

Her heart ached for him, but there was nothing she could do about any of that. She could, however, help him with Jack. And that's why she'd called her sister. A woman raising triplets who'd stood up to their dad and made a real life for herself out of nothing, Missy would know what to do.

"Did your car break?"

Althea winced. "Not that lucky. I got to Clark Beaumont's house early and he hired me immediately because his housekeeper has pneumonia."

"You're a housekeeper?"

"I'm just sort of helping out."

"Oh, Althea!"

"I'm fine. It's all fine."

Missy sighed. "No, it's not fine. You called me because you have a problem."

She grimaced. "Okay. Let me put it this way. It's fine that I got here early. I don't mind straightening up after breakfast and making sandwiches and opening a can of soup for lunch."

"But?"

"But the kids' mom was killed in an automobile accident three years ago. Teagan is only about three. Which means her mom died when she was an infant."

"Oh, that's awful."

She wanted to tell Missy that that was only half the Teagan story, but though Clark hadn't sworn her to secrecy she didn't feel right revealing intimate details of his life. So she stuck with the relevant facts.

"And Teagan doesn't speak. Well, she does. But she doesn't talk out loud. She tugs on her dad's or her brother's sleeve and whispers in their ears. They have to convey the message."

"Oh. Poor sweet thing."

"Clark thinks she's just shy."

"At that age, she could be."

"Yeah. I'm kind of waiting that out. The real problem is Jack. I'm here because Jack failed last semester."

"I know. Emily told me."

"Well, I don't think he failed because he's dumb or lazy or even because of mourning his mom, but because Clark is overprotective. He doesn't like the kids going into town because of gossip. He's got lots of money and a dead wife and two kids and he thinks everybody's curious about them." She grimaced at the sketchy explanation, but it was the best she could do without invading Clark's privacy.

"And you think Jack's failing is a cry for help?"

"If what he said yesterday when Clark sent

the police after us is true, I think it's a cry for freedom."

"He sent the police after you?"

She winced. "It all made sense at the time. I had taken the kids shopping without telling him. When he called and couldn't get us, he panicked."

"Althea, you've got a little girl who doesn't talk, a twelve-year-old who is rebelling and a paranoid boss who sent the police after you. Are you sure you want to get involved in this?"

"I have to get involved in this. If one person had paid a little attention to us, just one teacher or doctor or neighbor, we might not have spent every damned Saturday night in a closet praying Dad wouldn't kill Mom."

"Yeah." Missy sighed with understanding. "Okay. I get it."

Althea's shoulders sagged with relief. She knew her sister would understand that she couldn't abandon these kids. "So what do I say? How can I get Clark to understand that he can't protect Jack forever? That the poor kid just wants a little freedom? Maybe some friends?"

"Well, you could try explaining that kids are pretty resilient and even if the town is curious about them, once Jack's been in school awhile he'll be old news."

"That's great! I was also thinking of telling him that I'd like to use Jack going to school in town as an incentive for him to get his grades up."

"That's an even better idea."

"Good. I'll start working on him tonight." Happy with her plan, Althea shifted subjects. "So how are the kids?"

"Eager for Christmas. But Wyatt is worse. God only knows what he bought us this year."

She laughed. "You mean you didn't like last year's RV?"

"We love the RV, but the kids are getting spoiled."

"A little spoiling never hurt anyone."

Crazy Dog bounded out of the den and up the hall. "Crazy!" She flattened herself against the wall, and the dog whipped by her, but she pivoted and raced toward her again. "Crazy! You stop running right now!"

"What in the hell are you talking about?"

"The dog. Her name is Crazy. And trust me. She deserves it."

"Have you ever thought that maybe she'd behave better if she had a better, calmer name?"

Althea laughed.

"I'm not kidding. Call her Crazy, she'll act crazy. Rename that dog." She paused then yelped, "Owen! You stop that right now!"

Althea's laughter turned to fits of giggles. "I notice Owen's name doesn't make any difference in his behavior," she said, referring to the only boy of her sister's triplets. "I can't wait to meet them."

"Can you come for supper tomorrow?"

"I don't want to miss any interaction between Clark and the kids until I fully understand what's going on." She might know the whole story, but she wasn't sure how much Jack knew, how much he understood. "Give me a few more days to observe and analyze."

"All right." Missy paused to sigh. "But tread lightly, okay? You don't want to get in over your head. Or worse, this might be nothing and you could be interfering when you're not needed."

Knowing Clark had a right to be concerned, she let that comment pass. Crazy jumped up and licked her face, her big tongue making a slopping noise.

"And, Althea. Rename that dog. Give her a calmer name and maybe she'll settle down."

Disconnecting the call, Althea laughed. She petted the dog before shoving her off her shoulders and to the floor. "We're going to start calling you Lullaby."

The dog woofed.

She grabbed Crazy's collar and led her to the den. "All right. Maybe that one's a little too calm." She opened the door and Crazy broke loose, bounding over to the desk where Jack sat.

The force of her paws hitting the back of Jack's chair was so strong that she shoved Jack into the desk.

"Ouch!"

"Woof! Woof!"

"Crazy!" Althea patted her hands on her knees. "Get over here."

The dog bounded over and danced around her.

"My sister thinks we need to give the dog a calmer name."

Jack laughed. "A calmer name?"

"To make her behave."

"That's stupid."

"Yeah, but at this point I'll try anything." She glanced at Teagan. "Anybody have any suggestions?"

Teagan blinked. Jack sighed. "We already did this when we got her. We're not good with naming dogs."

"You have to think of something that sort of makes sense for her personality."

"Dad said Crazy Dog works."

"Yeah, but I think it just encourages her to be bad." Hearing what she'd just said, she frowned. Jack was right. It did seem stupid to change a dog's name and hope to change her behavior, but this pup was so big and gangly that Althea was desperate. "How about if we think about a name that describes how we want her to behave?"

"You mean you want to call her Angel?"

She glanced down at Crazy and she woofed.

"She'll never be an angel. She's more like the class clown." She paused and smiled. "You know, we could give her a clown's name so she'd still be allowed to be funny, but she wouldn't have to be crazy."

Jack laughed. Teagan smiled.

Althea tapped her fingers on her chin. "The only clown name I can think of is Ronald Mc-Donald…or Clara Bell."

As if testing the name, Jack said, "Clara Bell."

Crazy woofed and danced around again.

"I think she likes it."

Althea stooped down. Using Crazy's collar she brought her face up to hers. "Okay. From here on out, you are not Crazy. You are Clara Bell. You get to be fun but you're also a lady. Okay, Clara Bell?"

Clara Bell woofed then raced out of the den.

She and Jack exchanged a look. "I don't think it's going to work."

"My sister's pretty smart. If anybody's dumb idea could work, it's Missy's."

Jack rose and stretched. "So what are we going to do today?"

"I thought you were already working."

"I don't feel like studying right now. I want to do something fun."

She thought of dangling the chance to go to school in town as incentive to get him to work, but bit her tongue. She couldn't do that until she talked to Clark.

Then inspiration struck.

"Hey, if you spend the four hours you're supposed to spend at the computer and let me do a quick review with you, we can hang Teagan's wreath this afternoon."

Teagan bolted upright in her chair, her face glowing with excitement.

Jack sat again. "Okay."

"Okay." And now she knew a little incentive worked very well to motivate Jack.

Driving up the lane to his house that night, Clark narrowed his eyes. Something hung on his front door. He drove closer and groaned.

A big, gaudy wreath.

Anger skipped across his nerve endings, rippling to every part of his body, like waves from a stone thrown into a lake. After everything he'd told her the night before, she still left the house? Took the kids to town? Risked Brice seeing Teagan?

Grabbing his bags of fast food, he lunged out of his SUV, marched to the door and stared at the wreath. A huge circle of pine created a bed for red and gold ornaments. The ribbon of the big gold bow at the bottom cascaded along most of the lower half of the door.

It was, in a word, ugly.

He opened the door and stepped inside. After setting the fast food bags on the foyer table, he slid his scarf off his neck. Frustrated, he wondered why he'd bothered exposing his humiliation to her, if she had taken his kids to town anyway.

"I'm home."

Teagan barreled into the foyer, Crazy on her heels. She caught his arm and tugged until he leaned down.

He smiled. "What?"

She whispered in his ear.

His eyebrows rose and he winced. "*You* picked out the wreath?"

Her little head bobbed what seemed like fifty times in three seconds. Crazy woofed. Teagan caught his hand and turned him in the direction of the door. As he opened it, Althea appeared in the foyer, wearing jeans and a fuzzy pink sweater.

His prickling nerves caught fire and he froze.

Her yellow hair floated around her. Her summer-blue eyes sparkled. Everything male in him locked in on her.

Okay. Maybe the ugly wreath wasn't her fault, but this attraction was. Not that he was blaming her for his being attracted to her. But she was pretty... No, gorgeous. And obviously he was susceptible.

Teagan grabbed the door and opened it the whole way so they could see the wreath from inside the house.

Clark desperately struggled to corral a wince. "That's really some wreath."

A grin split Teagan's face, lit her eyes, wrinkled her pert little nose. The pride in her expression about tore his heart in two. Still, he'd asked Althea not to take the kids into town and she'd disobeyed him. He couldn't let that go. If she didn't obey his wishes, he couldn't keep her...no matter how good she was with the kids.

He caught her gaze. "So you took the kids to town again today?"

Arms crossed beneath her enticing breasts, Althea strolled over. "No. We bought the wreath yesterday when we were out."

"Oh." With no reason to be angry with her

anymore, he was totally defenseless against her charm. She stopped in front of him, and his hormones jumped and popped. His tie suddenly felt too tight. The room grew unbearably warm.

Her blue eyes glittered with happiness as she dropped her hand to Teagan's shoulder. His daughter, who rarely spoke and most certainly didn't cotton to strangers, looked up at Althea with a wide grin.

His breath stuttered. Teagan was relating to her? Not just relating, but coming out of her shell?

The happiness that invaded his heart nearly burst its seams. Joy circled through his system like a cyclone, creating a feeling so intense it stole his breath.

Oh, no! This wasn't just about an attraction anymore. *He liked her.*

Damn it! What was he doing? He didn't want to like her. He didn't want to like anyone! He had problems. Tons and tons of problems. All caused by the first woman in his life. The last thing he needed was to get involved with another.

Lights suddenly cut across the front yard. Teagan spun to face them. Crazy barked and raced out of the house.

"Crazy!" He turned to go after her, but Teagan caught his arm and pulled him down.

"What!"

She whispered in his ear.

He gaped at her. "The dog's name's not Crazy anymore?"

Althea winced. "Sorry. We thought if we called her something calmer than Crazy she'd start behaving. So we renamed her Clara Bell."

Sliding past him, she ran out after the dog. "Clara! Clara Bell! Stop."

Shaking his head, Clark stared after her. Crazy bounded through the snow like the Easter Bunny on steroids, woofing and jumping. Althea couldn't get close enough to grab her collar but she kept trying. And she kept calling poor Crazy Clara Bell.

Teagan giggled.

Clark glanced down at her. "I see renaming the dog worked out really well."

Teagan giggled again.

Althea caught the dog before the big black SUV stopped in his driveway.

Afraid to leave her out there alone when he didn't know who was in the car, he told Teagan,

"You stay here." Then he walked across the porch and down the steps as the SUV door opened and a petite blonde jumped out.

"Missy!"

Althea dropped Crazy's collar, ran to the short blonde and hugged her.

Crazy went nuts.

"Crazy!" He yelped, running over to the dog and catching her by the collar. Teagan yanked on his sleeve. He bent down automatically then groaned. "I told you to stay inside! What are you doing out here?"

She whispered in his ear.

He squeezed his eyes shut. "I know you re-named the dog, but right now Crazy fits."

"I told Missy it wouldn't work."

Clark straightened away from Teagan to see the tall dark-haired man who had spoken. He extended his hand for shaking. "Wyatt McKenzie. Husband of the woman who came up with the idea for the new dog name. And Missy," he said, pointing to the sobbing woman hugging Althea, "is Althea's sister."

Clark shook his hand once. "Clark Beaumont. It's nice to meet you." He glanced at Althea and her sister as his uncontrollable hound bounced and barked, trying to get free to join the reunion.

Althea stood hugging her sister. His heart stumbled.

She was good to his kids. She knew his secrets. And now he liked her.

This was trouble.

Althea swiped at the tears streaming down her cheeks. Clinging to Missy, she said, "I can't believe you're here."

Missy whispered, "I kept thinking about the dog and the little girl who doesn't talk and the boy who just wants friends. I had to make sure that you weren't in over your head."

Althea sniffed a laugh. "Still protecting me."

"We always protected each other."

She thought back to their days in the closet, huddled together, hiding from their dad. She remembered pooling their money so they would always have enough for lunches and football games and clothes. They were a team, but she'd been so desperate and alone after Missy moved out that she'd forgotten that.

She squeezed her eyes shut. "I have missed you so much."

"Yeah, I know. But at least it hasn't been eight years since we've seen each other," Missy said, referring to their real reunion two years ago. Once Missy had found her, she'd hopped on one of Wyatt's private planes and flown to California. She wanted to be sisters again, and though Althea had been afraid to come home because of their dad, she'd missed her sister. They'd mended their fences and become close again through video calls. "Phone calls are nice, but there's nothing like seeing someone in person."

Missy pulled out of her embrace. "You have to meet the triplets."

She opened the back door of the SUV and three kids rolled out. Two wore pink jackets and white mittens. The little boy had on a Pittsburgh Steelers' jacket. Missy sighed. "How many times do I have to tell you not to get yourselves out of your booster seats?"

"Sorry, Mom."

"Sorry, Mom."

"Sorry, Mom."

Althea hugged each one of them. Though she'd

"met" them in a video call, feeling the warmth of their little bodies with each hug filled her with joy.

Then they spotted Teagan. With a yelp of happiness, they raced over to Clark and his daughter.

The first little girl, a brunette with big brown eyes, said, "Hi, I'm Lainie."

Teagan all but crawled up her father's leg. Clark bent down and scooped her up. "Sorry. She's a little shy."

Missy walked over. "Does she like chocolate cupcakes?" She lifted the lid on a basket of chocolate cupcakes with white icing decorated with red and green gumdrops.

Teagan's eyes widened. Her head snapped around and she whispered in Clark's ear.

"Yes. I think she's offering you the chance to have one." He motioned toward the porch. "But not until after you've eaten dinner."

He caught Wyatt's gaze. "I bought fast food for tonight but I can head back to town and get a few more hamburgers and fries."

"No need." Missy motioned for her husband to go to their SUV. "I have a nice supper of lasagna and homemade bread in warmers in the back of our car."

Tears filled Althea's eyes again. Her heart stumbled in her chest. She hadn't seen her sister in two years and suddenly here she was with cupcakes and lasagna. Althea's two favorite things.

As Missy and Clark and the triplets headed for the front door, Wyatt grabbed a big picnic basket and followed them.

The men and kids walked into the house without a backward glance. But at the door, Missy stopped and faced her. "Are you coming?"

Althea pressed her lips together to keep from crying. Missy walked back, slid her arm across Althea's shoulders. "Are you okay?"

She caught her gaze. "I'm so sorry I left."

"We both did what we had to do." She squeezed her shoulder. "We've talked about all this. We're okay."

She nodded. They had talked about it. Missy understood that she'd needed to leave. She'd also understood Althea's fear about contacting anyone. And now they were beyond it.

"Besides, we're going to have fun tonight."

Wyatt yelled. "Hey, get in here already. I'm

sure Clark doesn't want to spend good money heating the outdoors."

Happiness bubbled through her. *Her sister was here.* She was about to eat lasagna and a cupcake. Jack would probably die of happiness having other kids to talk to, even if they were only six, half his age.

Then she looked at Clark just as he glanced over at her. Her heart warmed. Her pulse fluttered.

She might be close to her sister again, but with her other unresolved issues, was it wise to be falling for her boss? Especially when he appeared to have more troubles than she did?

CHAPTER FIVE

WYATT SET THE big basket on the center island. Missy immediately dug in, bringing out a fat loaf of Italian bread and setting it beside the basket before she opened the thermal case for the lasagna. She pulled out the casserole dish and removed the lid of the steaming tray. The sweet aroma of sauce, cheese and Italian sausage filled the air.

Althea's mouth watered.

Jack came into the kitchen, Clara Bell on his heels. His gaze roamed the room, taking in all the people. "What's up?"

Althea turned to him. "This is my sister, Missy, and her husband, Wyatt, and their triplets."

His eyes widened. "Triplets?"

The kids' heads bobbed up, their gazes honing in on Jack.

Missy said, "This is Lainie, Claire and Owen."

Owen said, "Hey."

Althea said, "They came for supper." Then she laughed. "Actually, they've *brought* supper."

But before Jack could reply, Clark said, "Okay, let's get everybody's coats off. Jack, you get the dishes and silverware and set the table."

Jack headed toward the dish cabinet. Owen slid out of his coat, dropped it to a chair and followed him. "I'll help."

At first Jack looked confused and Althea held her breath. Though he was starved for company, a six-year-old might not be Jack's idea of a playmate.

But he shrugged. "Yeah. Okay."

Missy and Wyatt helped the girls with their coats, then grabbed Owen's from the chair. "Where do you want these?"

Clark said, "I'll take them." But as he reached to take the jackets from Missy, Clara Bell leaped up, grabbed the loaf of bread from the center island, whipped around and raced between Clark and Missy who were passing the coats. Three little jackets and two adult coats, complete with mittens and scarves, flew into the air. Two scarves fell on Clara Bell's back and went with her into the hall and foyer.

Clark yelled, "Crazy!"

Jack said, "I'll get her," and ran up the hall.

Owen scrambled after him. Two seconds later Clara Bell raced back into the kitchen from the right-hand door, apparently running the circle of hallway that ringed the downstairs, scarves billowing from her back, bread clamped between her teeth.

"Clara Bell!" Althea said, reaching for a scarf and missing.

Lainie and Claire giggled and reached for the scarves, too. When they missed, they bolted after Clara Bell. Jack and Owen rounded the corner into the kitchen and raced after them.

"Kids!" Missy cried. "No running!"

Wyatt said, "I'll get them," and headed up the hall.

Clara Bell burst into the kitchen again.

Missy grabbed for her, Clark grabbed for her, Althea tried to snag her collar, but everyone missed.

Teagan calmly stepped in front of her. Clark gasped and lunged for her, but before he could get her, Clara Bell stopped dead in her tracks and laid the bread at Teagan's feet.

Teagan grinned.

Missy said, "Well, Teagan. For a little girl who doesn't talk, you certainly have a way of getting things done."

Everybody laughed but Clark. He picked up the slobbered on bread. "Luckily, when I was shopping on Tuesday, I bought a loaf of bread."

Missy started gathering the dropped coats and scarfs. "Where did you want these?"

After setting the store-bought bread on the center island, Clark took the coats.

When he returned, Missy said, "Why don't we get everything set up and eat?"

Clara Bell said, "Woof."

Clark scowled. "Oh, no. You go into the family room while we eat."

As if she'd done it a million times, Teagan walked over, took Clara Bell's collar and led her away.

Claire, the only blonde in the triplets, said, "We'll help," and she and Lainie raced after Teagan and the dog.

A few minutes later, the food was on the table and the girls returned. Lainie said, "We washed our hands."

Teagan held hers up with a grin.

"And without being told!" Clark scooped her up, walked over to the table and began organizing the seating. Because there were only six chairs, he and Jack brought in three chairs from the formal dining room. He put the triplets by their mom, with Wyatt on Missy's other side. Then he directed Jack to sit at his left and Teagan to his right with Althea in the middle of the table between both families.

Nobody spoke.

Althea exchanged a look with Missy, who smiled. "Why doesn't everybody just pass their plate up to me and I'll dish out the lasagna and we'll pass the plates back?"

Sending the plates around the table got everyone talking again. Realizing the bread Clark had bought on Tuesday hadn't been cut, Althea jumped from the table to do it. Comments on the delicious aroma of the lasagna swirled around. By the time she returned to the table with the bread, her plate of food was in front of her.

Jack took a bite of his food and groaned. "This is fantastic."

Missy grinned. "I'm glad you like it."

"My sister loves to cook. In fact, she owns a company that makes cakes."

Teagan's eyes widened.

Clark forked a bite of lasagna, but before he ate it he said, "Teagan loves cake."

Missy smiled at her. "Then I'll leave all the spare cupcakes here for you."

She grinned and nodded.

Clark frowned. "Is that good for her?"

"One cupcake a day for a few days won't hurt her."

Jack laughed. "Hear that, Chai Tea? You'll look like a cupcake when you're done."

Mouth full of lasagna, Owen giggled.

Lainie said, "Oh, gross." But Jack and Teagan laughed.

Clark shifted on his chair and addressed Missy. "Althea tells me you own your bakery."

"Yes. But I leave the management to a team. I'm so busy with the triplets that I save my work time for baking two wedding cakes a month. Because that's the part of the job I love."

He faced Wyatt. "And you do what?"

"I own a company that produces graphic novels."

Clark laughed. "No kidding."

Wyatt peeked over. "You like comic books?"

Jack perked up, too. "Only yes."

"Great. I'll have my office send up a few that won't be out until spring. You'll both be ahead of your friends."

Jack high-fived Clark and Althea's heart warmed. Two days ago, Jack wouldn't have been so open. Clark probably wouldn't have, either.

When his gaze met hers, she smiled at him.

He slowly returned her smile. Small lines crinkled around his eyes. And something happened inside her. A weird shifting. For as many problems as they had between them, she couldn't deny she liked him. A lot. Way more than a smart woman would like someone she'd known only a few days.

"Why doesn't Teagan talk?"

That question came from Lainie, Missy's little brunette with big brown eyes.

Missy said, "Hush now. She's shy."

But Teagan grinned across the table at the triplets, almost refuting Missy's words.

"She *is* shy," Clark said, "but that's because we live out in the country. She doesn't see a lot of people."

Little blonde Claire frowned. "She doesn't have friends?"

"There's really been nowhere for her to meet friends."

Owen shook his head. "That's sad."

"Owen identifies," Missy explained. "He used to sneak into Wyatt's house, looking for company."

"Too many girls in our house," Lainie said and rolled her eyes.

Wyatt laughed. "He just wanted some guy time."

Althea looked over at Jack. He looked back at her. A silent understanding passed between them. He wanted friends. No. He *needed* friends.

"Maybe you should send her to preschool," Missy suggested.

Clark didn't answer. He couldn't. The strangest things were happening. He hadn't had company in this house since his wife's death and it should have felt odd, uncomfortable. Instead, once everyone got over Crazy stealing the bread, the mood became warm and happy.

He'd even smiled at Althea, which was a huge mistake. Every time he looked at her heat rushed through him. But now, she wasn't just a gorgeous woman, living in his home, she was a nice woman with a sister who loved her and a family. In one silly meal she'd gone from being his son's teacher to being a person.

Which would be great, except the more he got to know her the more he liked her.

And he didn't want to like her.

He'd vowed he'd never get involved again. And he was a man who kept his vows. So why was she tempting him?

The two families finished the meal talking about snow and Christmas. Clark and Wyatt supervised the triplets and Jack loading the dishwasher, as Missy and Althea spent a few more minutes at the table.

Reminding their kids they had to get up for school in the morning, the McKenzies packed up to leave. Teagan hugged the girls. Jack and Owen made plans to meet online to play some kind of video game. Missy and Althea clung to each other.

Wyatt shook Clark's hand. "We'd love to have you come to our house next week."

He winced. "I'm kind of busy, but Althea's free to visit any evening. Every evening."

Obviously disappointed, Wyatt said, "Oh. Okay. That sounds great."

Clark felt like a real heel, but he absolutely positively couldn't get any more involved with Althea than he had to be for Jack's sake. His wife had more than broken his heart. She'd humiliated him. He wouldn't risk that again.

But when Althea said good-night as he and Teagan walked to the steps for bed, her smile was so radiant that his stomach clenched. For three wistful seconds he stared at her, wishing his wife hadn't cheated, wishing he'd known she was unhappy, wishing they'd gotten a divorce like a normal couple, wishing he wasn't scarred, bruised, wounded.

But that was foolish. He was what he was. Wounded. And he did have troubles. Troubles that kept Jack at home and Teagan away from prying eyes. He'd spent three years protecting his daughter. He wouldn't drag Althea into that.

Althea got out of bed the next morning, brushed her teeth, combed her hair, and did something she hadn't done in at least ten years. She put on makeup before breakfast. Not a lot. Just a little mascara and some lip gloss.

She studied her reflection, unable to believe she was so attracted to Clark Beaumont that she'd resort to makeup.

But she was. And he was attracted to her. She'd known that from their first handshake, but after the way he'd smiled at her at dinner the night before and the look of longing he'd given her before he climbed the stairs to take Teagan to bed, everything felt different. He liked her. And for once in her life she didn't want to run. She wanted this.

She walked into the kitchen, her long chenille robe tied tightly over her boxers and tank top. Clark and the kids sat at the center island.

She breezed to the coffeemaker. "Good morning."

Out of her peripheral vision she saw Clark look up. His gaze went from the top of her combed hair, down her puritanical robe to her bare feet.

She smiled. He was looking as interested as she'd thought he was the night before.

And she was very glad for the mascara.

"So what's everybody doing today?"

She turned from the coffeemaker just as Clark rose and put another pancake on his plate. His white shirt fit his firm chest very nicely. His orange-and-brown-print tie brought out the amber color of his eyes. But it was his tidy brown hair that sent a thrill through her. This was a normal, decent guy who was interested in her. Not a beach bum. Not a guy who got drunk and beat his kids. A guy who *protected* his kids. The kind of guy a woman could make a life with.

If she didn't screw it up.

If he really was interested.

If he was thinking the same way she was.

If they actually fell in love.

That was a lot of ifs.

"I have work. Two big meetings." He waited for her to bring her coffee to the open seat across from his at the center island. "I know it will be a long day for you guys, but that's the way it is when you own a company."

When she looked into his eyes her hormones went crazy, but he was back to being overly polite and cautious with her. Which, given that they'd basically just met a few days ago, was probably a very good thing.

She glanced down at her coffee to break eye contact. She had weeks to work this out. There was no sense rushing things. In fact, it was wise not to rush things.

Clark said, "How about you, Jack? What's on your agenda for today?"

Althea quickly glanced at Jack, who froze at his father's question.

"You know, neither of you has ever reported on what you're doing."

Jack's expression became defiant. "I'm working."

"I know you are," Clark said. "I'm just curious about how far you're getting."

Althea peeked at Jack's plate and saw it was clean. His breakfast eaten, he could leave. "Jack, why don't you go into the den and set everything up. I'll be in in a few minutes."

He sighed and slid off his stool. Teagan slid off her stool, too. She walked over, tugged on Clark's sleeve until he bent down, and hugged him. She didn't whisper in his ear. She just hugged him. Then she followed Jack out of the room.

For as closed off as Clark was with everyone

else, he certainly had a special relationship with Teagan. "She's something."

Clark's gaze meandered over to her. "Yes. She is."

"She has a heart full of love."

He sniffed a laugh.

"And so does Jack."

"I totally agree. His problem isn't personal. His problem is his schoolwork."

Althea stirred her coffee. "I was thinking about that yesterday, considering what I've seen in the past with the kids I've taught in a regular classroom, and I think I have an idea for an incentive to get Jack working."

His gaze met hers slowly again and this time her cheeks warmed. Of all the men she'd met in her life, happier guys, why did this man with closed off emotions make her breath stutter?

"What's your idea?"

She smiled to take some of the sting out of what she was about to say. "I think Jack needs company. Competition. Maybe even friends to toss around ideas."

"And you think I can go to the friend store and pick up a few twelve-year-old boys?"

She laughed. Okay. He'd made a joke. Maybe he wasn't so closed off after all. "No. I think we could inspire Jack to work harder, get his lessons caught up, if we told him that if he passed the required tests we'd put him in school in town next semester."

Clark's face fell. "What?"

"He's lonely. He wants friends. School is the obvious solution."

"I don't want him in school and you know why."

"But if we don't give him something to look forward to he's never going to perk up. But more than that he *needs* friends."

"He doesn't need to go to town."

"He does!"

"Damn it, Althea! We talked about this!"

She shut up. All thought of having a romantic relationship with him fell out of her brain. Closed off emotionally was one thing. Anger and yelling was another. She'd had enough of that from her dad to last her a lifetime.

Clark squeezed his eyes shut.

Damn it! The last thing he wanted to do was hurt her. He liked her. He actually wanted to do a lot more than like her. But this was exactly why he couldn't. His life was a mess and he didn't want to drag her into it as a girlfriend or lover or anything beyond Jack's teacher. "I can't send Jack to school in town because of the gossip. I don't want him to hear that about his mom."

Her eyes softened with understanding. "I know that, but that was three years ago. Kids in sixth grade won't be talking about it."

"But the teachers will."

"Who cares? They'll whisper about it for a week or so and it will drift away because your wife is gone. It's over and done. There's no fresh information."

He groaned and shook his head. "And what about Teagan? If Jack goes to school, he'll hear the gossip about her."

"Clark—" Her voice was soft again. Soft and full of sanity. "He's going to have to deal with this sometime. You can't keep him here forever."

He rubbed his hand across his mouth. "I know."

"Most people will be too kind to talk about it when Jack's around."

"Hopefully."

"Plus, he's mature for his age. He's a good boy.

A smart kid. Even if the gossip gets to him, you'll be able to talk him through it."

Clark drew in a long, slow breath. Jack had failed a semester, shouted that he felt he was in a prison. Was keeping him home doing more damage than letting him go to school?

"You could also ask the teacher or guidance counselor to watch out for him…to let you know if there's gossip so you'll be ready."

He looked at the floor, then back at her again, suddenly wondering if it really was Jack he was protecting…or himself. "I haven't really talked with him about his mom since she died." Sadness rattled through him. Because he hadn't known how to talk about Teagan, he hadn't talked about any of it. "Bits and pieces here and there. But nothing serious." He sucked in a breath. "Maybe if we talked about her…" He shrugged again. "You know, if I dropped a few normal things into the conversation like what she liked for breakfast, that could pave the way for the 'big' conversation we may someday need to have."

"I think that's a great idea. You're going to be talking about this sometime. So it would be good to start small. With normal stuff. Maybe even talk about Christmas things. Did she decorate?"

"Yes. But she didn't let anybody help. There are no memories."

"So that's what you tell him. You say, 'your mom loved to decorate the house so much she did it herself.' Then if he has any questions or wants to talk, you've opened the door."

He nodded. "Makes sense." He sighed heavily, scrubbed his hand across his mouth. "Okay. You tell him that if he gets his grades up, I'll look into sending him to school in town next semester."

CHAPTER SIX

JACK ABOUT DIED of happiness when Althea told him about her talk with his father. He dove into his studies, set the table for their lunch of canned soup and bagels and met his father at the door when he returned from work that night.

He launched himself into his arms, hugging him. "Thanks."

Clark's gaze rose to meet Althea's, as he spoke to his hugging son. "This is all contingent on you getting your grades up."

Jack stepped away. "I know. I will."

Althea slid her arm around Jack's shoulder. Looking at Clark she said, "So what'd you bring for dinner?"

"I stopped at a fish place."

"I didn't see a fish place in town."

"That's because I don't work in town. I moved my office to a big, empty warehouse in between Worthington and Greenfield, the next town over."

"Oh." And she knew why. He'd kept Jack out of school to protect him from gossip, but he'd moved his offices so he didn't have to deal with it, either.

"So, Jack, get the plates. I'll open the boxes and we'll have dinner."

They ate their fish, laughing over the fact that they would soon run out of fast food places to get supper. When dinner was over, Clark tossed his paper napkin into the basketlike container that had held his food.

"At least we never have to do dishes."

"I would do the dishes tonight," Jack said, happily gathering the boxes and paper bags to toss into the trash.

Althea caught Jack's arm to prevent him from leaving the room. "I have a better idea."

Clark peeked up at her. "Oh, yeah?"

Her nervous system went haywire. Now that they'd talked, she understood why. His heart had been on his sleeve that morning. He loved Jack but he was afraid. Not for himself but for Jack. To a woman who had grown up in a home with a dad who hated his children, Clark's love for his son was amazing.

She rose from the table. "I found a stash of Christmas decorations in the attic while Teagan was napping and Jack was working. I thought we could hang the lights."

Clark's face scrunched in confusion. "It's too early to put up a Christmas tree."

She gave him a look, trying to tell him to keep up with where she was going with this. They'd talked about him decorating with the kids that morning so he could interject things about their mom as they decorated. She was helping him get that ball rolling.

"I don't want to hang lights on a tree. I want to hang them on the porch, around the railing and along the roof overhang."

Jack cheered, Teagan clapped but Clark gaped at her. "You want to use a ladder in the dark?"

God, he was thick! Of course, he had worked all day and lots of things had happened to him in between this morning's conversation and now.

Still giving him her remember-our-talk-from-this-morning-look, she said, "There are plenty of outside lights on the front porch and around the house. Once we turn them all on, it won't be dark. Plus, there's a big storm coming on Saturday. We do it tonight or we don't do it at all."

Jack said, "Please. Please. Please."

Teagan looked at her dad with a pleading expression and Althea burst out laughing. He might have forgotten their conversation, but the kids wanted to decorate. "You're outnumbered."

He pushed back his chair and rose. "I'm also the one who's going to have to climb the ladder, which will be sitting in snow."

"We can anchor it."

Clark sighed. "Yes. We can."

Jack said, "Yay!" Teagan danced around, hugging her bear. Clara Bell woofed.

Clark shooed them all toward the front foyer. "I've gotta change into jeans. You guys get coats and boots on."

Jack helped Teagan with her coat and boots while Althea raced to the attic and retrieved the boxes of lights she'd found.

By the time she slid into her coat and boots and carried the two boxes marked Outdoor Lights onto the front porch, Clark was lugging the ladder over.

"Okay, ma'am, where do you want this?"

His imitation of a handyman made her laugh, but he wore the same tight jeans and sweater he'd had on the day she'd arrived at his house and Althea remembered why she'd instantly been attracted to him. The soft denim of his well-worn jeans caressed his butt. The sweater accented muscles hidden by his white shirts and ties. He looked happy, comfortable.

Her quilted jacket suddenly became too warm. She licked her lips.

"Althea? Ladder?"

Embarrassment flooded her cheeks. She'd been staring at him—virtually salivating over him—and he'd seen.

She peeked up, saw his twinkling eyes. Oh, yeah. He'd seen.

She shook her head haughtily, causing her hair to cascade around her. He wasn't the only attractive person in this equation and she wasn't the only *attracted* person in this equation. If he wanted to play games, he could bring it. She was ready.

"Are there hooks on the roof for the lights?"

His face contorted a bit as he thought. "If memory serves, I think there are."

She sashayed over, patted his forearm. "Then why don't you just take the ladder to the left corner?" She smiled sweetly. "You climb up, I'll hand you the lights and you can connect them."

His breath hissed out from between his teeth. He looked about ready to say something, but glanced at his eager kids and walked the ladder to the far corner of the house. He anchored the bottom before he slowly let it fall to the porch roof.

She smiled. "Want me to hold it while you climb up?"

He frowned. "I don't think we have a choice." Then his eyes narrowed. Probably because he realized she'd have a perfect view of his behind while he ascended the rungs.

She laughed. "Just start climbing."

As he ascended the first few rungs, she handed Jack the big circle of lights. When Clark got about halfway, they unwound enough of the string that he could take the end with him. He found the hook and latched it.

"It looks like there's a hook about every four feet. The next time I'll set the ladder in between two hooks."

"Makes sense to me."

He climbed down. They moved the ladder. Althea and Jack took a few steps to the right as Clark ascended again. This time he connected the lights onto two hooks.

That process continued until the front porch roof had been strung with lights.

Clark climbed down from the ladder. Teagan yanked on his sweater sleeve. She whispered in his ear and he shook his head. "We don't turn them on until we have all the lights up."

Her little lips turned down into a pout.

"That's what Mom used to say."

Clark's head jerked up and his gaze flicked to Jack.

Althea held her breath. Sympathy for Jack mixed with the ache she felt for Clark. He didn't want to talk about Jack's mom, but he had to. They'd already decided that this morning.

A second ticked by. Two. Three. Four. Five.

Then Clark quietly said, "She was a stickler for details."

The breath Althea had been holding leached out slowly, soundlessly. But she picked up some snow and tossed it at Clark. This couldn't be a sad conversation. It had to be fun. "Like you're not?"

Stunned, Clark pivoted to face her. She nudged her head in Jack's direction, hoping he'd catch her meaning. Nobody wanted to be sad. Three years had gone by. Jack needed to remember his mom in a good way. A happy way. Especially when it concerned a holiday.

"Oh, his mom was worse." Clark picked up the second string of lights and pointed so Jack would walk with him to the far side of the porch railing. "If you think I worry about details, you should have seen your mom."

Jack laughed.

Unstringing enough of the lights that he could latch them into the hook on the porch railing, he said, "She didn't like to shop in stores or malls. So she'd go online and pore over descriptions of silly things like ornaments for the tree as if they were family heirlooms."

"Someday they will be family heirlooms," Althea reminded them. "Jack, you and Teagan should find ornaments you really like, things your mom bought, and save them for when you're adults. They'll be great keepsakes for your trees."

Jack nodded.

Althea's and Clark's gazes met over Jack's head. Clark said, "You know, we don't talk about your mom much. Is there anything you'd like to know? A memory you'd like to tell us?"

He shook his head. "I don't remember much."

Althea placed her hand on Jack's back and rubbed affectionately. "Maybe you have photo albums?"

"We have some pictures on the computer," Clark said slowly. The subject was painful, but necessary. Still, even understanding that, Althea could see how difficult this was for him.

Teagan sidled up to Althea and slid her tiny white mittened hand into hers as she snuggled against her side.

Clark unstrung enough of the lights to get to the corner of the porch. Jack followed behind him, holding the neatly wound circle of lights. They worked together as if they'd done this a million times, but from what Jack had said about their Christmases they only put up a tree. Which meant these lights had been wound by his mom, Clark's wife. *That* was probably what Clark was remembering.

A reverent hush fell over the night. Surrounded by darkness, the lit porch felt like a world of its own. Clark latched the lights into the hooks. Jack followed him, the circle of colored bulbs unwinding as Clark walked it to the next hook. Teagan held Althea's hand.

She understood why Clark hadn't wanted to talk about his wife. She understood why he'd let a tradition or two go to the wayside. But the damage left in the wake of his necessary healing process was the emptiness, the quiet, the *silence* that seemed to permeate everything they did.

And she didn't know how to fix it. Her own life had been a dark place. Silent while her dad worked. Filled with terror when he was home.

Why had she ever believed she could help these kids? This family?

She might be attracted to Clark and she might long for a real relationship, but her problems had formed her. She'd never been anything but afraid, skeptical, wary. She didn't trust. She didn't know how to be a normal woman, forget about being a mom. And if she got involved with Clark, fell in love and married him, she instantly became a mother. Her only example of marriage was a man who beat his wife until she so feared her husband she didn't eat and died before she turned fifty.

Her thoughts that morning about having a relationship with Clark had been selfish and foolish. It might have been fun to daydream about it, but he had enough problems in his life without dragging him into hers.

When the lights were strung, they made a production number out of the official porch lighting. Teagan, Jack, Clara Bell and Clark stood in the snowy front yard, while Althea shoved the plug into the electrical outlet. Multicolored globes burst with color.

Clark's nerves crackled a bit as the first good memory of his wife rolled through him. She'd always loved Christmas. Decorated everything but the kitchen sink.

He laughed softly. "Your mom loved decorating."

Jack whispered, "I remember."

Teagan stood beside Jack. She slid her mittened hand into his. Clark saw, and his chest tightened. Teagan knew absolutely nothing about her mother.

He stooped down in front of her. "And your mom loved you."

She blinked at him.

"You were a tiny bundle of joy. She'd wanted another baby after Jack, but years went by before we got you." He swallowed, refusing to think about the fact that it might have taken another man to get his wife pregnant. "And when you arrived it was better than Christmas."

She grinned.

He scooped her up. "Now, let's go make hot chocolate."

"None of that junk you make with water in that silly coffeemaker of yours," Althea said, while they tromped through the snow to reach her. "I'm making real cocoa."

Clara Bell bounded ahead, racing to the front door and pausing to wait for Althea to open it. They walked into the house laughing. Jack's curiosity and sadness about his mom abated as he helped Althea make the chocolate syrup they would ultimately mix with milk.

Clark removed Teagan's coat and she smiled at him, as if in approval that he'd finally talked about her mom.

The tightness that always squeezed his chest loosened a bit. Althea cued up Christmas carols on her phone, put it on speaker and filled the room with magic.

Magic.

For the first time in three years, his house felt like a home.

They drank their cocoa. Jack excused himself to go to his room to watch TV. Teagan wrapped herself around his neck and he inhaled the sweet scent of outside that still clung to her, realizing he'd never taken the kids out to make a snowman or snow angels or to have a snowball battle.

But now he could. Now he would.

"You ready for bed, Chai Tea?"

She giggled, but she also yawned.

His gaze wandered over to Althea's. He wasn't stupid. He owed this—being able to take the next step—to her. But he'd also noticed, at a certain point while they were outside, that she'd shut down. She still helped with the lights, but she'd been the one to suggest she push in the plug. She'd said that the family should stand together in the yard and see the lights come on together.

Almost as if she didn't want to be with them. Didn't want to feel part of things.

But she was.

"Do you want to help put Teagan to bed?"

She shook her head, smiled slightly. "Like Jack, I think I'll watch TV."

"I was actually hoping you and I could have a chat."

"A chat?"

He caught her gaze. "Like we had this morning."

"Oh. Okay."

He knew she thought he wanted to talk about Jack and he supposed he did. But he also intended to find out what had happened out there. Why she'd shut down.

He bathed Teagan, read her a story, tucked her in and came downstairs about thirty minutes later.

He found Althea in the den, flipping through the channels on the big-screen TV. She hit the power switch as he walked inside. "I think that went very well."

"Thanks to you." He glanced around nervously, not knowing where to sit. The only chairs in the room were at the desk. Everybody sat on the sofa when they watched TV.

But she was sitting there…

And he was feeling things that he probably shouldn't, a closeness that warmed his soul. He wasn't a hundred percent sure that was a good thing, considering that he was ridiculously physically attracted to her. Still, up until that morning he'd thought sending Jack to school in town would be bad. Now he knew it was necessary, a crucial step in their healing.

Plus, she'd flirted with him. She'd tossed her hair, put her hand on his forearm, all but told him she'd be looking at his behind while he walked up the ladder.

He laughed. Good grief. He'd made it through a decorating session talking with Jack about his mom, the wife who'd betrayed him. Sitting by a woman he liked might not be a logical next step but there was nowhere else to sit and he was done being an idiot.

He plopped down beside her. "So what happened out there?"

She peeked over. "You decorated with your kids and talked about their mom?"

"No. I meant with you."

"Me?"

"Everything was going fine. You were a part of everything, nudging us along, making our conversation about Carol happen and then you suddenly shut down."

"I didn't want to intrude too much. It was your family moment. Something you guys needed," she said, sounding logical and honest, but he'd been there. He'd seen her sort of back away.

"I'd buy that if you hadn't seemed so sad."

She faced him. "But it was sad. I could all but see the heaviness around Jack's heart."

"And I could all but see the heaviness around yours."

Just as he saw it now. Her usually bright eyes had dimmed. Her always smiling mouth was a thin straight line.

He reached over and touched her hair before he even realized he was thinking about doing it. "Althea," he said her name softly, intimately. "I've told you things I've never told another person. And it's helped me. It's only fair you give me a chance to return the favor."

She licked her lips and closed her eyes.

And he knew he was right. Something big troubled her.

"I've never talked about this with anybody."

"Good. It'll put us on even footing."

"I don't even know where to start."

"Start with why decorating seemed to make you sad."

"Because my mom would try to decorate every year and my dad would come home drunk and tear down the decorations, as he called her names like worthless and lazy."

"Oh." That stunned him. He'd thought she was about to tell him about an ex-boyfriend who'd dumped her. Hearing her dad was a drunk shifted his perspective so far he couldn't quite comprehend it. "I'm sorry."

She sniffed a laugh, rose and walked across the room.

She had wanted to tell him the whole story, so that he'd stop looking at her with love and respect. Yes, she'd helped him with Jack, but any good teacher could have made the suggestions she had. If it came to them dating, falling in love, or her caring for the kids like a mother for any reason, she would fail miserably. So maybe it

was time to disabuse him of any fairy-tale notions he was getting because she'd figured out
Jack needed to go to school.

Pacing away, so she wouldn't have to look at
him, she said, "He would beat her. Usually every
Saturday night. Missy and I would huddle in the
closet and pray he'd pass out before he killed her."

She turned then, needing to see his reaction.
She needed to see the pity that would anger her
and force any romantic notions *she* had out of
her head, force her to move on.

But his face stayed calm, impassive. "And no
one helped you?"

"We were very good at pretending nothing was
wrong. Even after he started beating Missy and
then me, we could pretend we were fine in public. Missy was so perky and popular at school
she was voted everything from class president
to prom queen."

"You led a double life?"

"*She* led a double life."

He laid his arm across the back of the couch.
"And you?"

"I was the class clown."

"Ah."

She smiled slightly. "Probably the reason I identify with Clara Bell."

He laughed.

"I left home the day I graduated high school. Didn't go to my graduation ceremony."

His eyebrows rose.

"I pretended, just as we always did. I got dressed. Kissed my mom." Tears sprang up. "Joked a bit with my dad, accepted the money gift my sister gave me." She swiped away a tear that fell. "Then when we arrived at the high school, I got out of the car and headed for the entrance to the gym that the graduates were to take. But I didn't go in. I hid behind a corner and watched Missy and my parents walk to the main entrance. Once they were in the building, I ran back home, grabbed the suitcase I'd already packed and stole my dad's car."

He sat up. "What?"

She laughed a bit. "I didn't have a car and I had to get away."

"You're a felon?"

She laughed again. "Yeah. I guess. But I was also mad. I left the way I did so that they'd be in the audience, waiting for me to step up and take my diploma but I wouldn't be there. I wanted them to be publicly embarrassed that I was gone. And they were. Missy said our dad about blew a gasket. I drove to California and got a job so I could support myself through college."

"And you made it and your sister has forgiven you. I saw her face the other night. She clearly loves you."

"Yeah, but I didn't tell you the worse part."

"There's a part worse than your dad beating you?"

"My mom died the week after I graduated." The tears rose again. This time she let them fall. "I had no idea. I wanted so badly to be free that I didn't even try to get in touch with anyone to let them know I'd arrived safely. I hated them. I hated my dad for beating me and my mom for letting him and I wanted no part of them. Then two years ago, after Missy and Wyatt got married, she finally found me and told me that she loved me, that she wanted me in her life. I was thrilled because I'd grown past all the hate I had for her, but then she told me Mom had died."

The one attempt she'd made to save herself had

backfired. It brought more pain and guilt than her father's fists ever had.

"She died without me. I never got to say good-bye. I never got to say I was sorry because for all my big talk about her never trying to rescue me, I never tried to save her, either. Missy did. When she graduated from high school she went to the city and got a job as a secretary. She rented an apartment and let me stay there almost every weekend through high school so I'd be out of danger. She tried to get Mom to go, too, but—" She stopped, sobs erupted from her. She couldn't catch her breath. Didn't want to catch her breath. She wanted to be sad. She wanted to be angry. She wanted to find her dad and slap his face for being who he was. For keeping her from her mom. But in the end she was the one who had gone. Stolen a car. Broken her mother's heart.

The next thing she knew Clark's arms were around her. "I'm so sorry."

Sobs rattled out of her. "I could have called Missy at her office and let her know where I was. But I'd stolen a car. *Stolen* it. I was afraid that if I called, Dad would somehow figure out where I was and he'd send the police after me."

"You were desperate."

"I was *selfish*. I wanted out. I got out. I got on with my life as if I didn't have a care in the world and never knew my mom was dead until two years ago."

His arms tightened around her. "Shhh. That was a long time ago. And you were a kid. A desperate kid. My God. Your dad beat you."

Her only answer was a shuddering sob. He hugged her tighter. For the first time in her life she felt the warmth of true protection. He held her the entire time she cried. Cried for her mom. Cried for her sister. Cried for herself. For the little girl who had just wanted one normal Christmas.

"Do you know we never had a Christmas tree survive past Christmas Eve? My dad would always come home drunk and knock it down. He'd call us selfish for wanting gifts. Sometimes he'd find the things my mother had bought us and burn them in front of us."

Clark's breath hissed out. "He was an ass."

Her tears began to subside. "He was a bully."

"Exactly."

She pushed back, out of Clark's arms, but he

caught her shoulders and studied her face. "I'm not letting you go until I know you're okay."

"I'm never going to be okay."

"Don't be silly."

She shook her head, stepping away from him. "That's actually my point. I don't know what a good relationship looks like. I dated beach bums and losers because that's where I felt I belonged. My example of a mother is someone who fears her husband. The longest commitment I ever made was to the school where I taught, and even they got rid of me." She swallowed and looked up into his solemn amber eyes. "I don't know how to be what you need."

"Stop that." He reached for her but she ducked away from him.

"You and your family are wonderful. And you deserve much, much better than me. What happened out there while we were decorating, the part where I flirted?"

He nodded.

"Forget it. Forget anything you think you might have felt. You deserve much, much better."

She slipped out of the den and Clark stared at the door long after she closed it.

It was funny. He was thinking exactly the same thing, except in the opposite.

She deserved better than him—better than a family with a little boy who'd been overprotected, a little girl so shy she didn't speak and a father who wasn't even sure he was really a father because the wife he adored had betrayed him.

So though he didn't agree with her assessment that he deserved better, he would stay away from her. She deserved to find a man who didn't come with a houseful of problems. A man who wasn't even sure he could trust again.

CHAPTER SEVEN

ALTHEA LET AN entire week go by, waiting for Clark to resume decorating with his kids. Though the house wasn't quite as quiet and the kids were perkier, she knew they needed another burst of special attention. Thursday passed, then Friday with no offer from Clark to decorate again.

She came into the kitchen on Saturday morning a bit after nine, made a cup of coffee and sauntered to the center island where Clark and the kids sat having breakfast. The French doors displayed big white flakes of snow as they fell on the mountain. Another storm had arrived.

She set her mug of coffee on the island, across from Clark. "We have some evergreen garland and some ornaments we want to hang today."

From behind the screen of his laptop, Clark said, "That's nice."

She pushed his screen closed. "You're helping."

Jack laughed. Teagan grinned.

One of his eyebrows rose. "I am."

"Christmas is about family."

"I'm still three bids behind."

"So drop out of submitting on one of the projects and spend today with your kids."

He wanted to scowl. She could see it in his eyes. But she also knew he realized she was right. What they'd done the night they'd hung the lights was a good beginning. But he'd fallen down on the job.

"Jack, I pulled all the Christmas decorations from the attic. They're in the hallway by the attic door. If you and Teagan could start carting them down that would be great."

Jack took one final bite of cereal and headed for the door. "Come on, Chai Tea."

Bear in hand, she followed him. Clara Bell trotted after her.

"Exactly how much decorating are we going to do?"

She held back a smile. "I have terrific plans."

"I don't want to put up the tree until Christmas Eve."

"I'll give you that. But that still leaves garland on the stairway and around the doors of all the downstairs rooms. You have a fireplace." She began ticking off items on her fingers. "Which will need stockings."

He sighed. "There are stockings in the boxes."

"I know. I found them. I also saw red replacement shades for the lamps." The good mood she'd had while helping them string lights returned. But this time it was tempered with intelligence. She wasn't in any way, shape or form fit to be a mom. She also wasn't whole or healthy enough to have a relationship with a great guy like Clark. But that didn't mean she couldn't enjoy Christmas. "I found red and green placemats in a thin box marked End Tables so I'm guessing they go on the end tables in your living room. Then I thought the kids and I could take whatever is left over next week and decorate the den."

He shook his head. "What is it about women and decorating?"

"I don't know about other women, but I've never had the chance to decorate a whole house before."

"Oh."

Damn it. She didn't want him feeling sorry for her. But she had sort of led them down this path again. She lifted her chin. "Okay. So I've never had a real family Christmas. But I'm here with a family now, so I'm not going to apologize for enjoying it."

"Good. Then I won't apologize for letting you decorate." He rose from the center island. "That is, after I help hang the garland."

"Yes!" She fist-pumped once, grabbed her coffee and followed him out of the kitchen. Jack and Teagan scurried down the stairs. Teagan held a little box marked *manger* and Jack carried a bigger box marked Assorted Ornaments.

"Did you get the box marked *garland?*" Althea asked as she and Clark paused by the steps.

"It's in there." Jack finished as he walked down the stairway and angled his head in the direction of the living room. "We carried all the boxes in there."

Clark found the container with the garland. He pulled out a long strand of fake evergreen.

Althea raced over and peered at it. "It doesn't look too bad."

Clark turned it over in his hands. "How's it supposed to look?"

"Real. I'm surprised your wife didn't buy real evergreen."

He turned it over in his hands again. "Looks real enough to me." He caught Althea's gaze. "Must have looked real enough to her."

"Must have." She walked over to the box marked Nativity Scene. "You and Jack hang that. Teagan and I will set this up."

As she and Teagan removed donkeys and sheep, shepherds and wise men from the box, she heard Jack say, "Why would you think Mom would buy real evergreen?"

Clark said, "She liked nice things."

"Oh."

"Pretty things," Clark expanded.

Althea's soul swelled. He was doing what he needed to do, telling his son about his mom, and it was coming more naturally now. "You remember how everything in the house had to be perfect?"

Jack laughed. "Yeah. I remember."

"And you couldn't run inside."

"I still can't run inside."

"Well, she was more of a stickler about it than I am."

Althea made a face and Teagan grinned at her. She turned to Clark and Jack. "What was her favorite color?"

Teagan's head whipped around and she gazed at her dad with rapt curiosity. Color was something Teagan understood.

"Pink." He paused. "No. She liked to wear pink but she really loved gray because it went with everything."

Althea laughed. "That's a detailed answer."

"Don't forget," Clark said as he pulled a string of garland between his fingers, straightening it out, testing its strength, "We build for a living. I remember her nixing colors in architectural drawings and replacing them with gray."

"Interesting."

"She said it was a way for the client or buyer to see the building's potential without being encumbered by somebody else's taste in color."

Jack said, "Huh," as if pondering that. Or maybe thinking about his mom.

The conversation died as Clark left to get the stepladder and then climbed up and began attaching evergreen garland around the doorway of the living room.

They worked quietly, but companionably. Teagan arranged the figurines in the manger then took them all out and started again. Althea smiled at her, letting her work at her own pace and do her own thing.

She glanced at Jack, looking like a cross between a little boy and a teenager. Above him on the stepladder, Clark hung garland. To see them, no one would know that there had been so much turmoil in this family only two weeks before. She might not have turned them around, but she'd helped.

Something sailed through her. Something that felt like joy. Her head tilted in confusion. Joy. She was *happy*. She glanced at Clark. He was happy, too. Talking about his wife seemed to have taken away some of the pressure of the situation.

Just as talking about her dad, about her past, about feeling like a fake, had lifted some of her burden, too.

Not all of it. She still had to go back to Newland. She'd probably see her dad. But she didn't fear it the way she had when she arrived at the Beaumont household.

They decorated for about two hours, hanging

SINGLE DAD'S CHRISTMAS MIRACLE

stockings, changing lampshades, finding the perfect spot for the eighteen-inch Santa Claus statue that said, "Ho! Ho! Ho!" when Teagan pressed on his belly. She gasped and snatched her hand back.

But Clark laughed and hoisted her onto his shoulder. "He's just here to see if you're naughty or nice. He won't hurt you. I think it's time for me to get some work done."

Jack deflated. "But it's Saturday. I want to do something."

"Now." Althea put her hand on his shoulder. The living room and foyer had been decorated. Clark had talked about Jack and Teagan's mom. It might only be noon, but he'd done his fair share with the kids. "Your dad helped for two hours. He still has work to do. But I have an idea."

Jack glanced up at her.

"Why don't we bake cupcakes after lunch?"

Teagan gasped.

Jack's eyes narrowed. "You said you can't cook."

"That's because I haven't cooked in a long, long time."

"Why not?"

"I lived alone. I had no reason to cook. But,"

she said, gathering up boxes and placing them on the stairway to take back to the attic on her next trip up the stairs, "my sister and I both did a lot of cooking and baking when we were teenagers."

Jack made a face. "Why?"

She ruffled Jack's hair, sucked in a breath and did something else she hadn't done in ten years. She talked normally about her dad. "My dad owns a diner."

Jack's eyes widened. "He does?"

"Yep, complete with old-fashioned stools and a jukebox."

"What's a jukebox?"

Clark said, "It's a thing that plays records."

"What are records?"

"Songs," Althea corrected. She gave Clark a slight push toward the stairs and his office. "Go. You're making things worse."

He kissed Teagan's cheek then handed her to Althea and jogged up the stairs.

Althea sighed with relief. "Good. Now that he's gone I can admit I'm not a hundred percent sure I can bake good cupcakes, but we'll get some kind of cake."

Teagan smiled. Jack laughed and led the way into the kitchen.

After eating a sandwich, she and Jack scoured the pantry not just looking for ingredients for the cupcakes, but also hunting for something to decorate them. Clark hadn't thought to buy gumdrops or sprinkles on his last shopping trip and apparently Mrs. Alwine didn't use them.

Still, she found everything she needed for cake batter and the recipe from her teenage years simply popped into her head as if she'd been using it every day for the past ten years.

"The memory is an odd thing," she told Jack as he helped her measure cake flour. "I haven't made this cake in ten years, yet I can recite the recipe as if I made it yesterday."

"My mom was like that, too."

"Really?"

"She remembered everything."

"Did she cook?"

He laughed. "No."

A stirring of happiness bubbled up in her. Up to now she hadn't cooked any more than Carol had, but right now she was baking cupcakes—

She squelched the happiness. What was she

doing? Trying to be as good as or better than a dead woman? So she could have Clark? So she could be these kids' mom? She already knew she couldn't. Cooking and cleaning were nothing compared to the emotional things these kids would need. Things she couldn't provide because what she knew of childhood and teen years was hiding in a closet.

Two hours later, Clark came into the kitchen. "Just getting a cup of coffee."

"But we need sprinkles."

Clark faced Jack. "Sprinkles?"

Teagan displayed a bare cupcake. It had been slathered with pretty white frosting, but compared to the cupcakes Missy had brought two weeks before it looked incomplete. No gumdrops. No color.

He rubbed his hand across his mouth. "I really should get back to work."

"It is Saturday," Althea reminded him. Though she'd sided with him when they were done decorating, it felt like time that he should be included again. "And you've worked two hours. It's time for a break."

"And you want me to spend it going to the grocery store?" He paused. "Oh, wait. I get it. You want me to go into town for dinner."

"Actually, I was thinking about making chicken for supper."

She swore she could see his mouth water.

"Making chicken?"

"My dad had this recipe for chicken that melted in your mouth. People from three counties raved about it."

"Do you have everything you need?"

She winced. "There's no chicken in the freezer."

He downed his coffee. "Okay. So I need chicken and sprinkles."

"Sprinkles will be in the baking aisle."

"Got it."

When Clark returned an hour later, he had chicken and sprinkles. He also had potatoes, frozen vegetables, milk, cereal, gumdrops, candy canes, bread and enough groceries for a week.

With Clara Bell dancing around them, he and the kids put away the groceries while Althea picked through the bags, looking for the things she needed to make dinner.

"That was a smart trip," she said, smiling at him over the top of the bag.

"Yeah, I figured that since I was in town I'd get the things we'd need for a week."

"You'd forgotten you needed to shop, didn't you?"

He winced. "Yes."

She patted his shoulder as she walked by. "Don't worry. You're actually doing very well for a guy who's accustomed to having a house-keeper."

"Yeah, Dad. You are."

At Jack's praise, his gaze met Althea's over the shopping bag he was emptying. She smiled her approval and everything inside him sprang to life. She liked him. He liked her. They worked like a team. Something he'd never done with his wife. She'd had her skills and jobs. He'd had his. Their life was more like a relay. When she had the kids, he worked. When he had the kids, she worked.

With Althea everything was homey, comfort-able. What he remembered a family should be. But she thought she didn't belong.

Pulling chicken from a bag, Althea said, "So, Jack, what's your favorite memory of your mom?"

Teagan crawled up on one of the island stools,

put her elbows on the marble top and her little chin on her fists.

Jack shrugged. "She liked watching movies."

Clark stopped pulling cans from the bag. "She did." Good memories came tripping back, surprising him. "She'd rent every kids' movie when it came out on DVD and on Saturday nights, we'd watch them."

He'd forgotten that. How had he forgotten the one night of the week she gave exclusively to them?

The ice around his heart melted a bit. He'd hated Carol for so long he'd forgotten how much he'd once loved her.

"Oh, that's so nice! So many days I wished my family would rent a movie."

His head snapped up, his gaze flying to Althea. Just as he was growing comfortable talking about his deceased wife, she was growing comfortable talking about her family.

"My dad usually came home from the diner late, though." She met his gaze and he knew what she was telling him. She wouldn't say he came home from work drunk because of the kids. She shrugged. "So we never did anything like that."

Anything like a family. She didn't have to say the words. He got what she was saying. But he also saw something else. The mere fact that she could speak of her family so calmly proved she was getting comfortable with them—her memories—her life.

After the groceries were on the shelves, he sneaked out of the kitchen, grabbed his coat and drove back to town. He didn't like being in town. Though no one gave him crazy looks anymore, he didn't want to risk the possibility of running into someone who would. But on his second trip to Worthington that day, his muscles relaxed. He walked into the video store and inspected the selection of movies as if coming to town was a regular occurrence. He found two he knew the kids would like, bought some popcorn at the counter when he paid for the movies and drove home. He hid the movies and the popcorn in the den and went up the back stairway to his office.

At his desk, he closed his eyes. She'd talked about her family. He'd gone to town twice in the same day. They were changing each other.

After a chicken dinner that really did melt in your mouth, Clark led them all to the den. He walked to the desk, opened the drawer and pulled out the two movies he'd rented.

Teagan clapped her hands. Jack said, "All right!" And Althea laughed. "Wow. Those are great. Thanks."

"Oh, you haven't seen the best part." He pulled out the containers of microwaveable popcorn.

"But we just ate."

"I thought we'd get Teagan in pj's and let Jack get his shower for bed then we'd watch."

She scooped Teagan off the floor. "Sounds like a plan."

They ate popcorn and watched the two animated movies about talking fish and dancing penguins. Teagan curled up in his lap and fell asleep. Jack cuddled in with Althea. With the four of them huddled together on the sofa, they looked and acted like a real family. Though part of Clark was happy he could give that experience to Althea, another part held back.

He knew what was happening. He was falling for her. And he couldn't. He shouldn't. For as much as he and the kids looked like a happy little unit now, there was trouble in their lives. Big trouble. Problems she shouldn't have to bear.

Even though she thought she was the one who didn't deserve to be part of this family, he knew better. *He* didn't deserve her.

He carried Teagan to her bed, said good-night to Jack at his bedroom door and returned to the den with a heaviness in his chest.

When he opened the door, he found Althea cleaning up the popcorn bowls. "That's okay. I'll do that."

"You've done enough for one day." Her eyes actually sparkled with happiness. "The decorating was fun. And you talked about the kids' mom again, which makes Jack so happy, but also seems to thrill Teagan." She picked up the second bowl. "Going for sprinkles won Teagan's undying love, but they flipped for the movies. It was a night they'll probably never forget."

She'd gotten all the bowls, so he busied himself picking up kernels of popcorn that had fallen to the couch, not wanting to meet her gaze. He didn't know whether it was good or bad that he so desperately wanted to make her happy. But the joy that shot through him was filled with male pride and *that* was wrong. He couldn't have her, and doing things for her might only hurt her when it was time for her to leave.

"Why don't you go on to bed?"

"In a minute." She sighed. "The night was nice for me, too. Fun." She sucked in another breath. "But I didn't mean to make you feel like you had to do nice things for me when I said I wanted to enjoy being part of a family for Christmas."

"I did it for all of us."

The grateful expression on her face nearly did him in. He wanted to walk across the room, take her chin in his hand, stare into her eyes and tell her she was beautiful, that she deserved someone to treat her with respect and make her a part of things. But the "things" of his family weren't simple like dinner or popcorn or decorating. They were big, difficult problems he and his kids would face. Maybe soon, if he sent Jack to school in town.

She deserved a man who would put her on a pedestal, not drag her down with even more problems.

She walked over to him. "You're a sweet man, Clark Beaumont."

He winced. "No man wants to be called sweet."

She laughed. A light, airy wonderful laugh that filled him with the same warmth he'd had that morning while decorating.

Her hand automatically went to his forearm and he realized how much she touched him, touched Jack, held Teagan. It was as if she was reaching for contact, *begging* for contact.

"You can be sweet and still be manly."

He laughed, but she didn't take her hand off his forearm and the skin beneath it radiated with warmth.

He looked into her big blue eyes. He wanted so badly to kiss her. To really kiss her. He wanted so badly to love her. To bring her into his home, share his life.

He knew he was two steps away from falling in love with her. But he also knew she deserved better...more. Someone who could love her totally and completely. He could not. Even if he didn't have problems, Carol had scarred him. He seriously wondered if he would ever trust a woman again.

He shifted her hand away. "Don't."

"Don't?"

"You might be too innocent to know what's going on here but I see it."

She gaped at him. "Innocent?"

"You are innocent. You had a terrible childhood so you hid from life."

"Clark, I'm also twenty-eight. I've had boyfriends."

He shook his head. "I'm sure you have, but I'm equally sure you never let yourself fall in love."

She grimaced. "That transparent, huh?"

"People with problems recognize other people with problems."

"Your problems are resolving themselves."

He shook his head, paced away from her. "You would think."

"Clark, I don't think. I *know*. Jack is totally different than when I came. Teagan is coming out of her shell. Before you know it she's going to talk. Out loud."

He sniffed a laugh.

"What? Are you still worried about the gossip in town?"

"Actually, I finally see that it's time to face the gossip in town. To let Jack hear the truth, if it comes out, and process it with him. So he can heal."

"But…"

He sucked in a breath, not wanting to say what she was leading him to but knowing that if he didn't tell her, she'd never understand why he had to stay away from her.

"But the problems with Teagan aren't so simple."

"You'll handle it the same way you're handling Jack. If and when she hears a rumor, you'll explain."

He walked to the desk. Ran his fingers along the shiny top.

"Clark, that's the only way to handle it. Honestly."

He met her gaze.

"What?"

"I can't be honest."

She stared at him. He could almost see the wheels turning in her head as she tried to understand that answer. Finally, she said, "You have to be honest."

"Sure. It'll be easy to tell her she's not my daughter."

She gasped. Her eyes widened and she gaped at him. "Why would you tell her that?" She stopped, her mouth formed an O of understanding. "Oh, my God. This isn't about gossips. This is about you. *You* don't think she's yours?"

"No. I don't."

She fell to the arm of the sofa. "Oh, Clark! You can't believe the gossip!"

He fiddled with a pen that sat on the desk. "My wife and I tried to have another child from the time Jack was two." He glanced over at her. "We couldn't."

"That means nothing! You'd already produced Jack. You weren't sterile."

"We barely slept together."

She squeezed her eyes shut.

"For the first year after Carol died, I waited for Brice to figure it out. To come to my house demanding to see Teagan or demanding a DNA test. He never did."

"So that's good!"

He shook his head. "No. He was preoccupied. He left his job working for me and had to find another—while he mourned the woman he considered the love of his life."

"You identified."

"I understood." He paced away from the desk. "About two years after Carol died, he got married. I thought he'd think of it then, but he never did." He glanced over again. "He has kids of his own now."

"You're saying you think he doesn't want her?"

"I'm saying I don't know what he's thinking, but I do know that if he ever figures it out, he'll come after her."

CHAPTER EIGHT

SYMPATHY FOR HIM created a tight band around Althea's chest. "You can't torture yourself with this."

"Of course, I can. Not just out of fear for myself, but fear for Teagan. Even if he never comes after her, she deserves to know the truth."

"But you don't really know the truth. You said you and your wife had made love a time or two."

He sighed. "A time…or two."

"So you could be Teagan's dad."

"The odds are slim."

"So get a DNA test yourself."

He strolled away, back to the desk Jack used to study and Teagan used for coloring. "Then I'll know."

"Exactly."

Anger brightened his whiskey-colored eyes. "Don't you see? I don't want to know! Once I know, I might have to face the fact that she's not mine. As long as there's doubt, she could still be my little girl."

"As long as there's doubt you'll worry."

"Better to worry than to know."

"But what if she's yours?"

"Did I tell you how small of a chance there is?"

"If she's yours, you won't ever have to worry about whether or not you should tell Teagan. You won't have to tell her anything."

"And if I find out she's not mine? What about then?"

"You'll figure it out."

He shook his head. "As long as I don't know then I don't have to face the fact that I might be keeping Teagan from her real father. Once I know I have to make some very difficult choices."

"Look, at some point you're going to have to tell her. Why not have the truth?"

"Haven't you been listening? The truth is the one thing I'm trying to avoid."

"Oh, yeah? How about imagining how you'll feel if you discover she's yours."

"So relieved I'll dance on this desk."

"Which is exactly why you should do it. You can't run from this. You can't spend your life worried that some guy from your past will waltz in and ruin your future."

"The night I came home from Carol's wake and was bathing Teagan for bed, I about exploded from fear. So I told myself to just get through the next few days and prepare myself to lose her. But Brice never came. And I never sought him out because I love Teagan. I'd watched her birth, walked the floor with her. She'd been my little girl for six months by then. I didn't want to give her up. I don't want to give her up now."

She walked over to him. "You said he moved on, but from the way you stay out of town, I'm guessing he still lives in Worthington."

"He does."

"And you live on a mountain so removed from everybody else that if it weren't for your job, you'd be a hermit. It's not good for you. Not good for the kids. You have to face this."

He ran his hands down his face. "I don't want to."

But even he heard the waning conviction in his voice. He'd held back from doing the right thing out of fear. Yet that same fear kept him hostage.

Kept his kids prisoners. They couldn't go on like this anymore. "I'll look for a lab online."

When Althea strolled into the kitchen on Sunday morning, the room was as quiet as the first day she'd arrived. Jack and Teagan stared into their cereal bowls. Unshaven, in pajamas and a robe, no computer in front of him, Clark stared straight ahead.

She set the coffeemaker in motion and faced the center island. "So, why's everybody so gloomy today?"

Jack shrugged. Hugging her bear, Teagan gave her a pleading look. Clark's gaze met hers slowly. The pain in his eyes melted her heart. Knowing he had to face the truth about Teagan was killing him and she suspected the kids were reacting to his mood.

And who could blame them? Their daddy was sad.

Holding her now finished mug of coffee with both hands, she strolled to the center island. "You know, the mall in Hagerstown is open for shopping today."

Jack's head jerked up. "You wanna go shopping?"

"I have to buy gifts for my sister and her kids. Maybe even something for Wyatt. I could use your help."

Clark rose from his stool by the island. "That's a great idea. You and the kids go shopping."

Teagan grinned, crawled down from her stool and hugged Althea's legs. Warmth filled her, along with a determination to make sure Clark didn't undo all the good he'd done the day before by being so solemn today. If it took getting the kids out of the house, away from him, that's what she'd do.

"I'll take Teagan upstairs and get her dressed."

Jack hooted and hollered. Clara Bell danced around and followed him up the stairs. In Teagan's bedroom, she found a warm sweater and jeans for the little girl and brushed her hair. The fine dark strands fell into place, but her bangs were too long to go without something to hold them out of her eyes. "You wait here one minute. I'm going to get you a clip for your hair."

She raced down the stairs, but when she reached the kitchen and saw Clark still sitting on his stool staring straight ahead, she stopped short. It wouldn't do him any good to stay home, either. Not if he spent the day moping. He needed to get out. Needed to get his mind off possibly losing Teagan.

"You should come with us."

He snorted a laugh. "Frankly, I want some time to think."

"Thinking is over. Decision is made. You're getting the test. So now you have a choice. Make everybody so miserable that you'll regret it if the results come back in your favor. Or make everybody so miserable that Jack will realize something is up and all the good you've done over the past few days will go down the tubes."

He sighed.

She walked over, put her hand on his shoulder. "You're not spoiling my first ever real family Christmas."

He sniffed a laugh.

"I'm serious. If this is your last Christmas with Teagan, you'll regret it if you don't make it wonderful."

He looked down at the center island, then back at her. "I may tell her when she's old enough to hear, but even if she's not mine I won't let her go. I'll fight for her tooth and nail. She's been with me for three years. He's never even thought to get a DNA test. And if he does, and he comes after her, I'll fight him."

She patted his back. "That's the spirit!"

He chuckled, but his stomach clenched. For the past three years, he had pretended everything was fine because he didn't know for sure that Teagan wasn't his. Once he got that test and discovered the truth, he'd be living a lie.

Still, Althea assembled the kids, got their coats, slid little boots onto Teagan's tiny feet and was waiting at the front door for him when he came downstairs. The second he stopped beside Althea, who held Teagan, Teagan pointed at the shiny red clip in her hair.

"What's that?"

She grinned.

"That's a clip I bought last year to wear in my hair for a Christmas party." She smiled at Teagan. "I think it suits the day."

He kissed Teagan's cheek. "I think it does, too." He shrugged into his coat. "So, we're going to the mall?"

Jack fist-pumped. "Yes!"

Althea laughed.

But Clark wondered if this was the first day of living a lie or the last day he could honestly pretend Teagan was his.

She crawled down, out of Althea's arms, and walked over to him. Raising her arms, she silently asked him to carry her.

He reached down, hoisted her up and she kissed his cheek. Warmth blossomed through him. Though he knew getting the DNA test was the right thing to do, he wanted this day. Every hour. Every minute. Every second.

They piled into his SUV and carefully headed down the snow-covered mountain toward town. Instead of driving along Main Street, he veered to the left, circled the little town and headed for the Interstate.

Sitting on the passenger's side seat, Althea slid a sideways glance at him.

He cleared his throat. "Interstate is faster."

She nodded.

The trip took an hour. In spite of the falling snow, the parking lot was jammed to capacity. Clark let them off at the mall entrance and found a parking space. He left his SUV so far back in the lot that by the time he reached them, standing in the center of the rows of shops for the outdoor mall, he was covered in snow.

In Althea's arms, Teagan leaned over and brushed the snow from his hair. He laughed. "Thank you."

She grinned.

He glanced around at the brightly lit stores, the garish decorations, the bustle of people. His stomach tightened. This was the place everyone from town shopped.

As if reading his fear, Althea reached over and tapped his forearm. "Where to first?"

He shrugged. "You're the one who needs to shop."

She glanced at Jack who had wandered away, toward the big front window display of an electronics store. "You need to shop, too. And this would be a great day to ferret out what a certain someone wants for Christmas."

Teagan grinned.

Althea pinched her cheek. "And you, too."

"So that's what this is all about?"

"That's part of it. While I check out things for

the triplets, you can scope what makes a certain three-year-old smile." She nodded at Jack. "I can go to the electronics store pretending to want something for Wyatt and you can see what games Jack gravitates to."

He loosened his shoulders. With a mission in mind, this shopping trip didn't seem so bad after all.

"So." She directed him to a store. "Let's start with finding something for the triplets." Looking behind her she called, "Jack, are you coming?"

He scrambled over.

Christmas carols blared through the store. A chorus of "We Wish You a Merry Christmas," followed them as they trudged to the back and the children's clothes.

Teagan on her arm, she stopped at a rack of little girls' holiday dresses. She pulled out a red velvet dress trimmed in white fur that made it look like something one of Santa's elves would wear.

"This is pretty."

Teagan smiled.

"Come on, this warrants more than a smile. It's adorable. I can see Lainie in it. And maybe the blue one for Claire with her big blue eyes and yellow hair."

Teagan frowned.

"Seriously?"

She scrambled down from Althea's arms. Althea expected her to go to her dad. Instead, she bolted off.

"Teagan!"

Instantly alert, Clark ran after her. Althea ran after Clark and Jack scrambled after her.

In and out of rows Teagan bobbed and weaved, so short it was difficult for Althea to keep track of her. But she could see Teagan was backtracking, going toward the front of the store. The door opened and closed. Althea gasped and raced toward it, knowing Teagan had gone outside. On the sidewalk, she spotted Teagan headed for a toy store. The little girl was too short to reach the door handle so she slid in when a pair of grandparents walked out. Althea, Clark and Jack bolted after her. They wound through rows of toys just far enough behind Teagan that they couldn't grab her. But she suddenly stopped at a doll display.

Althea screeched to a halt when she reached her. Clark followed suit. Jack stopped behind him.

Althea stooped in front of Teagan. "Never do that again."

She grinned and pointed at a doll. A baby wrapped in a pink blanket with a pacifier in her mouth.

"She's cute."

Teagan nodded.

She smiled, as an idea occurred to her. "Is this what you think the triplets would want? Owen might not appreciate that."

Teagan shook her head furiously.

"So it's for the girls?"

She shook her head again.

Althea peered up at Clark, who crouched down in front of Teagan. "Who wants this then?"

She pointed at herself.

"Oh, so *you* want it?"

She nodded. Her face came alive with a happiness Clark had never seen before. She didn't just like the doll. She liked being out. Seeing things. Shopping. Sadness crept over him. He'd deprived her and Jack of so much because he was afraid.

Though he'd realized the night before that Althea was right—he had to know the truth about Teagan—he felt it even more strongly now. His kids couldn't be hidden anymore. They had to have normal lives. Even if it meant that ultimately he'd have to fight Brice Matthews for custody of the little girl he considered his.

Lifting Teagan, he rose. "Thank you for telling me what you want, but you know I'm only Santa's ambassador."

She frowned. Her head tilted.

"You remember Santa, the guy in the red suit who brings the gifts?"

She nodded.

"Well, I'll tell him that you told me this doll is what you want."

Jack pointed to the back of the store. "Or she could tell him herself."

Clark's gaze followed the direction of Jack's point and he saw Santa. A tingly hope filled him. "Would you like to tell Santa yourself?"

Her eyes widened with fear and she buried her face in his neck.

Althea patted the little girl's back. "It's a nice idea, but it might be too much for one day."

"I was hoping…"

She smiled at him. "But today's not the day. Today's the day for looking around. Maybe getting some caramel popcorn."

Teagan's head snapped up.

Clark said, "If you're good."

She nodded furiously.

He laughed.

Althea browsed the toy section with Teagan following her around, pointing at gifts. Half she thought were good choices for the triplets. The other half she wanted for herself.

On the guise of looking for something for Wyatt, they strolled to the electronics store. Pretending not to notice Jack, they let him wander away. Though Clark stayed with Althea, the store was small enough that he could see everything that caught Jack's attention. He made mental notes of game names and gadgets. By the time Althea chose something for Wyatt and they walked out of the electronics store, everybody was shopped out.

Clark said, "How about we find the caramel popcorn and head home."

Carrying four huge bags, Althea agreed. "I've never spent this much money on Christmas before."

Clark led them to the vendor with the popcorn. "What did you do for Christmas before?"

"Normally nothing."

He held back a grimace. He should have known better than to ask that. He bought the popcorn and they headed down the long parking lot to the SUV.

They packed Althea's bags in the back of the SUV while it warmed up and then headed home. The big box of popcorn sat beside Teagan's car seat and she reached in and grabbed a handful.

"Hey, you can't have that until after lunch!"

Jack groaned. "But we're starving."

Clark winced. He'd noticed they hadn't eaten their breakfast. He'd been in such a black mood that no one had eaten. But his mood was so good now, his attitude so positive, that he caught Jack's gaze in the rearview mirror and said, "So let's stop in town for pizza."

Jack said, "All right."

The trip back to town flew by. He parked beside the pizza shop and got out of the car. When he opened the backseat door and began to unstrap Teagan, both Althea and Jack gaped at him.

"What? I thought it would be faster if we ate the pizza here."

Jack scrambled out of his seat belt. "Sounds good to me!"

Althea followed close after him. "Sounds good to me, too."

The scent of tomato sauce and warm crust greeted them as they entered the little pizza place. They sat at a table with a red-and-white checkered tablecloth, and Clark found a booster seat for Teagan.

The waitress came over. They ordered a large pizza with everything, three colas and a glass of milk. Then Althea got up and walked over to the old-fashioned jukebox.

"Here, Jack. This is a jukebox."

He walked over. "Oh. It's kinda weird. Why not just listen to your iPod?"

She laughed and fished out some change. "What do you want to hear?"

He shrugged.

"How about Christmas songs?"

They chose some music and walked back to the table. As they waited for the pizza, the little restaurant began to fill. Half the people who came through the door walked up to the high counter to get takeout orders.

Finally their pizza arrived and they dug in. Clark handed out slices to Jack and Althea, then cut a piece into tiny bites so Teagan could eat it.

With Christmas carols filling the air, and warm delicious pizza filling their tummies, everything was perfect. The joy of it filled Clark to bursting and he knew he owed Althea for this. Right at this moment, he could almost believe that when he got the results of the DNA test he would learn that Teagan was his. And the fear would be over. The niggling doubts that stopped him from enjoying his life, his kids, would be gone.

And maybe he wouldn't have to worry about dragging Althea into his troubles. He'd only have to worry about the fact that he couldn't trust.

But what better way to learn to trust than with a woman who constantly proved her worth?

After a quick supper of salads made from things they found in the refrigerator, Althea cleaned the kitchen, then joined Clark and his kids in the living room for TV. Shopping, pizza and making salads as a family had gotten Clark past his nerves and had turned Jack chatty.

But the day had been too much for Teagan and she fell asleep on Clark's lap. Gently cradling her, he rose from the sofa.

Althea rose, too, to help put the little girl to bed, but he stopped her with a wave of his hand. "I'll get her. You and Jack relax."

He returned in ten minutes, telling Althea that he hadn't bathed her, simply slid her out of her clothes and into pajamas. She nodded.

He smiled at her.

And her stomach plummeted. She couldn't describe the look in his eyes, the way his smile affected her, but she knew that—in her entire life—nobody had ever looked at her quite like that.

She turned her attention back to the television, her nerves tingling.

Ten minutes later, Jack yawned and stretched. "I'm tired, too."

As he walked past Clark, Clark grabbed his hand and squeezed. "Too much time walking outside."

Jack sniffed a laugh. "It was still fun."

"Yeah. It was."

Jack grinned, happier than Althea had ever seen him. "Good night."

She and Clark said, "Good night," and Jack left the den.

Althea turned her attention back to the TV. Out of the corner of her eye, she noticed Clark shifted on the sofa, bringing his knee up to the cushion so he could see her.

That's when it hit her that they were totally alone.

"I'm sort of tired, too."

She squelched a sigh of relief. She'd probably imagined he was looking at her differently. She faced him with a smile. "Good night, then." She pointed at the TV. "I'll turn everything off."

He smiled and nodded, but didn't get up from the sofa. Instead, he leaned toward her, caught her shoulders and pulled her to him. His lips met hers softly.

Her heart knocked against her ribs and she tried to slide away, but he kept her where she was, moving his lips across hers again.

Warmth exploded inside her. Her breath shivered out. She wanted to wrap her arms around his neck, pull him to her, and lose herself in him and the kiss that was so gentle and sweet.

But he drifted back. Smiled again. "Good night."

Then he left the room and she sat staring at the door.

Hadn't they decided they weren't going to pursue this?

CHAPTER NINE

ALTHEA COULDN'T BELIEVE he'd kissed her. The next morning when she got out of bed, her lips still tingled from it. She stared at herself in the mirror, equal parts of happy and confused. She knew he liked her. She liked him, too. But they were supposed to be smarter than to start something that wouldn't work.

When she walked into the kitchen, her gaze traveled over to him, and he smiled at her.

Her nerves twinkled like lights on a Christmas tree.

"So what are you guys doing today?"

Jack rambled off a list of his lessons as she made herself a cup of coffee.

When he was done, Clark turned on his stool to face her again. "So what are you going to do this afternoon?"

His beautiful, perfect smile could have lit the room. Her limbs froze, as real fear rattled through her. She didn't know how to be in a normal relationship. But she was already halfway in love with Clark. And she didn't want to run or hide. She wanted this.

"I think…" Because her voice cracked, she cleared her throat. "I think I'd like to go see my sister today."

One of his eyebrows arched.

Okay. So he'd figured out the kiss had rattled her. Wasn't honesty part of a real relationship? It was good that he knew.

"Do you want to take the kids?"

"I could."

He laughed. "Why don't you wait until I come home? Call Missy let her know you're coming tonight."

She nodded. A shivery feeling rippled down her legs, knocking her knees. She'd never wanted and feared something simultaneously. But looking at Clark's happy expression, seeing the kids eating their cereal and even Clara Bell jumping around, she knew she wanted this.

If it killed her she would get over this fear that she wasn't good enough.

Clark arrived home promptly at six. Handing

the keys to his SUV to her, he said, "I know you have a car, but I'd feel safer if you took this."

She glanced at the keys, then back up into his eyes. God, he had gorgeous eyes. And he was generous and kind and smart…

Okay. She was smitten. That's why she was going to see Missy. To learn how to deal with this. "Thanks."

He caught her by the shoulders, bent down and kissed her lightly. "Have fun."

She nodded, smiled at him and headed out the door, her knees knocking and her stomach clenched but her heart soaring. A real, normal man liked her. And she was already as close to loving him as she could be without actually falling. She could have a life…a home. A real home. With happiness and holidays. Safety and love.

The drive to Newland took an hour. Part of her wanted to squeeze her eyes shut as she drove through town, but practicality wouldn't allow that. So she drove through, eyes open, looking at buildings that hadn't changed much. The grocery store. The hardware. The library. She slowed Clark's big SUV, taking it all in.

It was like traveling back in time. Except, she

didn't experience the fear she'd expected. Even this close to the diner her nerves were steady. She passed the short wide building that housed her dad's restaurant and smiled. No fear. No weirdness. Lights still lit the diner, and customers still sat in the booths along the wall of windows.

She sucked in a breath. As long as she didn't go into the restaurant, she wouldn't see her dad. There was nothing to be afraid of.

A little farther down the street, she saw Missy's Bakery. Cupcakes decorated the big sign above the door of the little shop. Pride sizzled through her.

Missy had done it. She hadn't merely broken free of their nightmare. She'd started over. She'd married a great guy. She had her own business. She raised her kids without fear.

Awed, she pulled the SUV into the parking space in front of the bakery and got out. Shoving her hands into the deep pockets of her blue coat, she stared up at the pink-and-blue Missy's Bakery sign. She looked at the cute cupcakes, smiled at the wedding cake in the front window, thrilled with everything her sister had accomplished.

"Pretty impressive, ain't it?"

She gasped and her knees about buckled. Her short, stocky father stood right beside her. His hair had thinned out and life had worn lines in his face, but he still had the same air of superiority, the ability to instill fear.

"Our little Missy, all grown up. Becoming a big girl in this town."

She licked her suddenly dry lips and refused to look at him, while she plotted whether or not she could spin away and race back to Clark's SUV before he could catch her.

"Nice SUV you're driving."

"It's my boss's." She found her voice, if only to keep him from making incorrect assumptions about her.

"Fancy. What do you do these days?"

Everything inside her told her to run. She couldn't imagine why he was outside Missy's Bakery when the lights were still on in the diner. But that was how it went with her dad. There was never anywhere to run. No way to hide. It was as if he had radar and always knew where she was…unless she was three thousand miles away.

She mumbled, "I'm a teacher."

"Hump. Not as highfalutin' as your sister."

His attempt to goad her got lost in her fear. She told herself she didn't have to stand here and even talk to him, told herself no one would blame her for simply turning and walking away, so she did. She turned, walked to the SUV and opened the door.

"Still no time for your old man?"

Ignoring him, she climbed inside.

He shook his head and kicked snow like a little kid. As she pulled out onto the street, he waved.

Her hands shook so badly she could barely drive. She forced herself to focus and when she turned onto the street for the house where her grandmother used to live, the house where Missy and Wyatt now lived, her eyes bulged. Not only had a huge addition been attached to her grandmother's little Cape Cod, but the house next to it—the one owned by Wyatt's family—had also been remodeled.

She parked in the wide driveway, behind the huge RV, her heart in her throat. Every bad memory she had rolled through her brain. The fear. Her mother crying and begging. Missy reading to her in the closet, telling her not to be afraid, telling her someday they would get out.

Tears filled her eyes. Missy had gotten out.

And she had, too. As long as she was away from Newland, she was okay. Her tears fell off her eyelids and rolled down her cheeks. She pulled down her gearshift and silently let the SUV roll backward out of Missy's driveway.

Missy had always been the strong one. She wasn't strong. Fear still haunted her.

She didn't have to talk to Missy. She already knew she wasn't ready for what Clark wanted.

When Althea arrived home, Clark watched her take off her coat, completely confused. The red rims around her eyes told him she'd been crying. He'd expected her to come home happy, bubbly…

Ready.

For what he wasn't entirely sure himself. The kiss had knocked him for a loop. And she'd let him kiss her before she'd left that evening. He thought they were carefully moving toward something.

Maybe he was wrong?

Or maybe he was reading too much into this?

Except—he glanced at his watch—she hadn't been gone long enough to visit her sister. The

length of time was only enough to drive to Newland and turn around and drive back.

Now he was really confused.

Following her down the hall toward the kitchen,
he said, "Hey, you're back early."

She wouldn't look at him. "I changed my mind
about visiting Missy."

"Really?"

She said, "Yeah. The drive was fun. It was nice
to get out of the house but I wasn't in the mood
to talk tonight."

He stopped following her. Wasn't in the mood
to talk? He'd thought she needed to talk? That
that had been her purpose in going. "Okay."

She turned and smiled at him. "The drive was
relaxing, but I'm actually tired and I think I'm
just going to my room to watch a little TV."

"You don't want to help put Teagan to bed?"

She shook her head and walked down the hall
that led to her suite of rooms. A few seconds later
he heard the door to her room click closed.

He ran his hand across his mouth. What had
just happened?

She spent the week barely speaking to him,
though it didn't seem obvious because Jack talked

nonstop. From his constant chatter, Clark figured out that Althea wasn't skimping on Jack's lessons. If anything, they were pulling ahead and Jack was jazzed. His grades were up. His mood was good. He'd be going to school in town in January and Clark wasn't afraid.

But Althea was gone. Quiet. Not talking. Barely eating.

Something had happened on her trip to town and if it killed him he would get her to tell him.

Saturday morning, Althea woke later than normal. Worried about how she'd spend a whole weekend avoiding Clark, she dallied another twenty minutes in her room, waiting to hear the noise of him and the kids having breakfast, but she heard nothing. As the hands on her clock clicked toward ten, she told herself that she'd probably slept through their breakfast.

She ambled into the empty kitchen and made herself a cup of coffee. Before she could turn and go into her room, Teagan raced into the kitchen and over to her, plowing into her knees. Jack followed close behind her. Both kids wore their jackets and mittens.

"Are you going out to play?"

Clark walked into the kitchen. "No. They're going to my parents'." She noticed the pair of sixty-year-olds behind him. "Althea, these are Mona and Dave Beaumont. My parents. Mom and Dad, this is Althea. She's Jack's teacher."

His parents said, "How do you do," and smiled at her.

"It's nice to meet you."

His mother clapped her hands. "Come on, guys. We have to get going. Snow's coming again."

Jack said, "Bye," and pivoted away from her. Teagan smiled until Althea got the message and stooped down. Then she hugged Althea with all her might, spun away and raced to her grandmother.

Clark followed them out of the kitchen, but returned in what seemed like seconds.

"Already had the car packed," he said as he walked to the coffeemaker. He popped in a single serve packet and put a mug under the drip. "So they're off. I'm glad you got up in time to say goodbye."

The room fell silent as she processed everything. The kids were gone and they were alone.

Alone. Never once had he talked about the kids leaving for weekends. So why suddenly were they spending a weekend away?

Finally she said, "Is this a regularly scheduled visit?"

He pulled his now-full mug from the coffeemaker. "I thought the kids could use a break. My mom's always wanted to have them a weekend before Christmas to help decorate, bake cookies, that kind of stuff. But my parents live in town so that never happened. Anyway, now that I'm beyond that, I called her to see if she wanted them this weekend and she was thrilled." He looked at her over the rim of his mug. "Plus, I think you and I need to talk."

Fear about suffocated her. "Talk?" She should go to Missy's. She almost said the words, but remembered running into her dad and those words froze on her tongue.

"About what happened between us."

A wonderful kiss. The generous offer of his car. The way he let her go to her sister's. The easy, familiar way he accepted her.

Longing welled up inside her. He was the kind of man any woman would want. But she didn't fit into his life. Her father reminded her of that. A woman whose idea of love and marriage was abuse had no clue of how to be the lover of a man like Clark. A woman who'd spent her childhood hiding had no idea of how to be a mother to his children.

"I thought we'd kind of silently agreed our getting involved was a mistake."

He smiled over the rim of his cup. "I was giving you time."

She swallowed. "Time?"

"To think through whether or not you want to be involved with me."

Every fiber of her being yearned to. But she could hear the cigarette-roughened voice of her dad, talking about how successful Missy was. And the realization, standing beside him, that the only way she'd ever gotten free of him had been to run.

She would run again. Except this time she wouldn't steal a car or have only two hundred dollars in her pocket. As soon as her task with Jack was finished, she'd have a few thousand dollars. Enough to keep her while she sent teaching résumés to states like Texas or Idaho. States so far away no one would ever find her.

"I'm not who you think I am." She tried to smile at Clark, but knew her attempt had been weak at best. "I'm one of those people who does better alone."

With that she walked into her room and closed the door. The thought of being cooped up in the twelve-by-twelve space all day made her think again about going to Missy's. But she couldn't. She wouldn't. Not only did she not want to see her dad, but what if she drew her dad's attention to Missy again? What if he began harassing her?

She couldn't risk it.

She spent two hours sitting by a window in a pretty aqua club chair, watching the snow fall, and an odd memory surfaced. When it snowed like this, big, wet flakes, she and Missy had made snowmen. Living in California for the past decade, she hadn't even seen a snowman let alone made one. She suddenly, desperately needed to be out of this room, but more than that, she needed to do something. Something that reminded her of the one good thing she could remember from her childhood.

She had a coat, boots and mittens. So it wasn't as if she was ill prepared. Plus, Clark had undoubtedly retreated to his office to work. No one had to know. No one had to see her. And the kids would love the snowman when they got home.

She peeked out her door. Kitchen was empty. She could do this.

Clark glanced out his office window and burst out laughing. Unless he missed his guess, she was building a snowman.

Stretching, he rose from his desk and walked to the window. She looked adorable in her blue coat and black mittens, but something was wrong. Something big enough that she needed the physical diversion of rolling a huge ball of snow.

He left his office, grabbed his coat and shoved his feet into sturdy boots. He exited through the front door, so she wouldn't see him and sneaked up behind her.

"What are you doing?"

She spun to face him, her mittened hands flattened on her chest as if he'd scared the tar out of her. A reaction he found a little drastic.

"Are you going to tell me what's up?"

She swallowed. "I'm fine."

"Oh, hell, no. You're not fine."

Her chin lifted. "I am." She turned away and put her attention on the second ball she was rolling to be the middle of her snowman.

Okay. So the direct approach wasn't getting him anywhere. He sucked in a breath. The air was crisp but not frigid. Big white flakes of snow billowed around them. The silence intensified the peace in his soul. Peace she'd helped him find. Whatever was wrong, he wouldn't let her go through it alone.

But if she wouldn't talk—he stooped down, grabbed two handfuls of snow and packed them into one big snowball—then he'd just have to loosen her up.

Ten feet in front of him, she labored over her snowball, her butt in the air, her arms straining as she rolled it, gathering more snow.

He gave his big snowball one final pat before throwing it at her butt.

Thwack. Direct hit.

She shot up straight and pivoted to face him.

He bent and built another snowball. Before she

could say anything, he tossed it at her middle. It landed with a wet thunk.

Her eyes widened. "What the hell are you doing?"

"Loosening you up."

He bent again.

"Loosening me up? For what?"

Whack. He hit her again. This time in the thighs.

Her widened eyes narrowed. "Oh, you are so dead."

"I don't think so. I think you've been in California too long to be really good at a snowball battle."

She bent, gathered snow, threw it at him and missed.

He laughed. "See? I was right. Of course, anybody with any recent snowman experience knows that you don't roll the snowball that you have to put on top of your first snowball."

Thwack. She hit him right in the chest.

"You think I'm a lightweight?" She scooped up more snow. "I might have been in a warmer climate for years, but this isn't exactly brain surgery." She hit him again. "There's a very low learning curve on snowball throwing."

This time he was smart enough to duck away from her snowball. It whizzed past him. As he ran, he bent and scooped up more snow. He turned and tossed it at her. Direct hit.

She didn't waste a second. Chasing him, she gathered snow. He lost sight of her when he ducked around the side of the house. He stopped, flattened himself against the wall and worked to slow his breathing. When she flew around the side, he caught her arm and pulled her to him.

The stunned expression on her face had laughter bubbling from him. He breathed in the fresh air, savoring this one precious, wonderful moment that he knew he'd remember forever.

He wasn't afraid. He wasn't angry. He wasn't unhappy. He was with somebody who made him laugh.

"I think this is against the rules of the Geneva Snowball Convention or something."

He laughed again. His heart swelled with a wonderful freedom that intoxicated him. Already holding her one arm, he hooked his hand around the second so he could pull her closer. He didn't give her two seconds to realize what he was about to do. He swooped down and kissed her.

Thoroughly. The way he'd wanted to kiss her from the second she'd shaken out her pretty yellow hair. He moved his lips across hers roughly, but enticingly, feeling her yield beneath him.

The world around them became a reverent hush as he realized he was falling in love again. Differently this time. Not with a partner. Not with a friend. But with…someone he adored.

He wasn't quite there yet. He was wise enough to hold back a bit. But he was on the brink.

When her hands crept up his arms and slowly slid to his neck, he smiled against her mouth. Unless he missed his guess, she was falling, too. Their lips moved against each other, tongues mating in the silent world.

But she suddenly pulled away. Stepped away. Turned away. "Don't."

He reached out to catch her shoulder and force her to face him, but she shrugged him off.

"Okay. Fun and games are over. I like you and you like me. Why are you rejecting me?"

She said nothing.

He put his hands on his hips and looked up at

the snow that fell to his face. "You know what? You were a bit shaky but agreeable until your trip to your sister's." He paused, frowned. "Who you never actually visited. What the hell happened?"

She still said nothing.

"Do you want me to get another snowball?"

She peeked back at him. "I was winning that fight."

"In your dreams. If I'd wanted to destroy you I would have." He took a step toward her. His voice softened. He ran his hand down her knit cap to the yellow hair that peeked out beneath it. "What happened that night? Tell me. Maybe I can help?"

She sniffed a laugh. "Right. That's exactly what my dad wants. He wants you to feel sorry for me. Then he can swoop in and tell you his sob story so you'll give him money. Or maybe he'll blackmail you and just demand money."

He held up his hand. "Wait! What are you talking about?"

"The night I was supposed to visit Missy, I stopped on Main Street when I saw her adorable little bakery. I couldn't believe it and had to look at it close up."

"I get that. You're proud of her."

"Yeah. It was great until suddenly my dad was standing beside me."

"Oh."

"He liked your car by the way. He guessed you must have some money just from the look of it."

"That doesn't mean I'm going to give it to him."

She snorted in derision. "Oh, you don't know my dad. He's a con man and a bully, remember? Once he finds a mark, he doesn't let go."

"And you consider me incapable of calling the police?"

She sniffed a laugh. Peeked back at him again. "You'd just call the police?"

"You are talking to the guy who wouldn't take his kids to town for three years." His chest puffed out with pride. "I take care of my own."

She laughed.

"You told me to think positively about Teagan. You told me not to let gossip or negative things get me down. Now I'm up because of you. I'm ready for whatever happens. You can't wallow in misery, when you wouldn't let me wallow in misery."

She laughed again as a funny feeling assaulted

her. She gave herself a second to examine it and realized it was hope. She faced him. "This is a little more than wallowing. He's going to come after your money."

He shook his head. "Let him try."

She pressed her lips together, drew strength from his strength, confidence from his confidence. After all, her dad was fifty miles away. Why should she cower now?

"I still think I won that snowball battle."

He put his arm across her shoulder and led her back to her two big snowballs that would eventually be a snowman. "Yeah, but I won the war." He kissed her again. Happiness bubbled inside her. This was what sharing your life felt like. She knew it. She'd never had it before, but there was no mistaking the feeling.

He broke the kiss. "Let's finish the snowman and surprise the kids."

She nodded. Pieces of her broken heart began to knit together.

He bent to pick up her second snowball. With a grunt, he lifted it and put it on the first snowball. "You think you could have lifted that alone?"

She shook her head. "No. Not alone." And

maybe that's what life was all about. Realizing you couldn't do the heavy lifting alone.

"Want some hot chocolate?"

He grinned at her. "Yeah. But we've got one more layer of snowman. Then we have to find him a hat…and some eyes. Maybe some twigs for arms."

"You've done this before."

"Everybody's done this before."

Maybe everybody had, but it was the first time she'd shared something with a man, something that though not intimate was personal. She tucked the memory away. She was still scared. She was still vulnerable. She knew she could—would—make huge mistakes that might send him running, but today he was hers.

That afternoon, she shooed him out of the kitchen so she could make dinner. All the cooking lessons her father had given her came rolling back. Except this time, her fear didn't resurrect. Clark was right. If her father came here, if he tried to blackmail her, or even have her arrested for stealing his car, she would deal with it. Actually, as soon as she got the money for tutoring Jack, she would give her dad a certified check and make him sign a paper saying that was a total payoff of her debt to him.

She smiled. Now that Clark had her thinking logically, she was thinking very logically.

While her pork chops baked she raced into her bedroom and began a search for attorneys. She intended to pay her dad the money for the car, but she didn't want to be afraid anymore. She needed to get him to sign something. So he'd never have anything to hold over her head again.

Twenty minutes later she returned to the kitchen to check on her scalloped potatoes and pork chops. The entire room smelled divine. Like a home. Her home. She set the table by the French doors so they could watch the snow fall. She found candles and dimmed the lights so the snowfall would be even prettier. More romantic.

When Clark walked into the kitchen and saw the candles, he stopped. "Wow."

Nerves invaded her. "You don't like it?"

His gaze ambled to hers. "I think it's very romantic."

"That was the look I was going for."

"You're okay with this?"

She laughed. "First you push. Now you're pulling back."

"I'm not pulling back. I just want to make sure I'm not pushing too much."

"You're not."

But when they were on the couch in the den that night, watching an old movie, and his arm slid across the sofa, over to her shoulders, warmth tingled through her along with a shiver of fear. He was so special. He deserved a wonderful love in his life and she knew…she just *knew* that she'd screw this up somehow if they went too fast.

Using his arm around her shoulders, he pulled her closer, snuggled her against him. The dual reactions of fear and need spiraled through her. The temptation was strong to lay her head on his shoulder, close her eyes, just enjoy this.

Why shouldn't she? She might eventually ruin everything, but tonight he was hers.

She sucked in a quick breath, let her head lean to the right an inch, two inches, three inches…

"Dad!"

Clark bolted up. "Did you just hear Jack?"

She jerked away. "Yes!"

He popped into the room, Teagan on his heels.

"Gramma says she's sorry but she forgot about some Christmas cookie thing she has tomorrow."

Clark jumped up off the sofa. Althea slid to the far end before she also rose.

"Cookie thing?"

"I think she said it's an exchange." He grinned. "But she said we can come back next weekend."

"Next weekend is Christmas."

Jack laughed. "I think she knows."

Clark tossed her an apologetic look before he put his hands on the kids' shoulders and herded them toward the door. "It's late. You guys had a busy day. Time for bed."

When they were gone, Althea fell to the sofa, grateful for the reprieve. But deep down inside, she admitted she might have been lucky tonight. She wasn't ready for what her body seemed to want with Clark.

Still, she and Clark lived together. One of these nights he'd kiss her again, hold her again…

And though she wanted this, she wasn't ready.

CHAPTER TEN

THE NEXT MORNING when Althea strolled into the kitchen and stopped at the counter to make her cup of coffee, Clark could see she was nervous. He'd felt the tension in her the night before. He'd felt her stiffen when he'd put his arm around her while they watched TV.

But she also hadn't run. She might have been nervous, unsure, but she'd laid her head on his shoulder—albeit only for ten seconds before the kids came home.

"So, Grandma said that any night this week we could come back and stay over to make up for not being able to stay over last night."

"Sounds good to me."

Teagan clapped her hands over her mouth, her big brown eyes growing even bigger.

Clark smiled. "I'm surprised you're happy to stay away from the house without me."

She grinned.

Jack said, "She ate more cookies than she painted."

Althea joined them at the center island. "Your grandma makes painted cookies?"

"Santas and Christmas trees—" Jack counted off on his fingers "—bells, sleds, churches, elves. They're sugar cookie shapes and the paint is icing."

"I've made those."

Clark's chest tightened. She'd probably made those for her dad's diner. She was talking again, opening up, albeit slowly because she wanted what he wanted. A relationship.

He watched her fuss over Teagan's breakfast. She'd said she wasn't innocent, that she'd had boyfriends. But he had a sense that none of her boyfriends had been dads...or older than she was. Having a relationship with him was probably different than anything she'd done before. And for a girl who had been abused, different was probably scary.

He didn't intend to run from this, but he also wouldn't push her. This was as new for him as it was for her. They had plenty of time.

"Well, I'm going upstairs to the office." He

turned and headed to the door, but on second thought, he stopped. "I only want to work until noon, so what do you say we go to town and get pizza for lunch again?"

Teagan gasped and threw her hands across her mouth. Jack said, "All right!"

Althea perked up. "Now, there's a good reason for all of us to get out of our pajamas."

Althea and Jack played video games until it was time to get dressed to go to lunch. She took Teagan into her room and they poked through the drawers to find something cute to wear out.

"Did you keep the clip for your hair?"

She nodded and raced to her dresser. She lifted a little Cinderella figurine and produced the sparkly red clip Althea had put in her hair a few days before.

Her heart melted. Clark was doing the best job he could with these kids but from the way Teagan hid her clip, like a treasure she didn't want stolen, she could tell Teagan would love to be more girly.

"You know, while we're in town for lunch, we could pick up a whole pack of clips for you."

She nodded eagerly.

And maybe tonight she'd mention to Clark that they should take Teagan shopping for clothes, let her pick out some things. Right now she had nothing but T-shirts, sweaters and jeans in her closet. Maybe she'd like a dress?

With Teagan and Jack ready to go, Althea headed back to her room. She showered quickly and walked to her own closet. She rifled through hangers of sweaters and jeans, suddenly wishing she had something prettier, too. For the first time in her life, she wanted to dress up, look special, look feminine…not like the girlfriend of a guy who spent his life surfing. No bikini. No ripped jeans. No hoodies. She wanted to look pretty.

But since she didn't have anything but jeans, she found her neatest pair, slipped into a red sweater and hunted for the red clip that matched the one she'd given to Teagan.

When she stepped out of the hall into the kitchen, Teagan grinned.

She smiled at her. "We're sort of twins now."

Clark's face scrunched in confusion. "Why?"

She pointed at her clip. "I have one. Teagan has one."

"Oh. That's cool." He feigned excitement for Teagan's sake, and she suppressed a happy sigh. This was what she loved about him. He probably couldn't give a flying fig about matching clips, but he knew it meant something to Teagan, so he made a big deal out of it.

In a flurry of passing hats and finding mittens, they put on their outdoor clothes and headed to the garage and Clark's SUV. He strapped Teagan into her seat as Jack buckled himself into the seat beside her. Althea took her place in the passenger's seat beside Clark.

Behind the steering wheel, he smiled at her. "Ready for pizza?"

She nodded, smiling. Such wonderful, inconsequential talk. Like a real family. Like people who loved each other.

It might be too soon to be in love, but it wasn't too soon to behave like people who cared about each other. She was starved for it, intrigued by it, so enamored with the idea of being in love, being in a real family, acting like a normal person that her heart felt like it could explode.

Now if she could just get past the damned fear.

The drive to town took the usual twenty minutes. Clark got Teagan out of her seat. Althea made sure Jack was okay. They walked up the decorated street to the pizza place.

Warmth greeted them as they stepped inside. The waitress remembered them. Jack ordered the pizza, making Clark laugh and Althea relax. All this might seem special to her, but it was normal for a family. *Normal.* And if she could relax, be herself, this could all be hers one day.

They sipped their soda and chatted about Jack's schoolwork for the twenty minutes it took for the pizza to bake. It arrived with a flourish. Napkins and paper plates were passed. Clark cut Teagan's slice into tiny pieces. The waitress brought second sodas.

Other customers finished eating and left. New customers arrived and filled the seats around them. They ate their pizza. Clark paid the bill, and they walked out onto the street.

Althea didn't want it to end. She wanted to walk up Main Street again, see the decorations with Clark and the kids, enjoy the brisk air, talk about nothing some more.

"You know, Teagan's hair looks great with the red clip, but there are lots of colors she could wear. In fact, if we got some hair ties, I could put her hair in pigtails tomorrow or a ponytail."

In Clark's arms, Teagan gasped. Clark frowned. "Would you like some hair ties?"

She nodded.

He smiled. "I think most of the shops are closed today, but if Althea doesn't mind, she could bring you back tomorrow and get them then."

She froze. He would let her take the kids to town...on her own? He'd made such great strides in letting go of his fear that Althea was bolstered by his success. If he could let go of his fears and accept that the kids needed breathing room, then surely she could put her fear about a relationship aside.

"The drugstore's open."

Clark and Althea glanced down at Jack.

"It is?"

"Yeah and it's got the girly stuff in it."

Clark peeked over at her for confirmation.

"Drugstores always have makeup and clips and hair ties." She grinned. "Girly stuff. We could get her clips now." Which would extend their trip, helping her adjust to the fact that she fit here. With this man. His kids. In their life.

"Okay. Then let's go to the drugstore."

The wind whipped up as they walked to the very end of Main Street. A brand-new brick building housed the popular chain store. Althea pulled her jacket hood up over her hair as they walked across the almost empty parking lot and the wind swirled around them.

She held the door open for Clark, who still carried Teagan. Inside, they all stomped their feet on the mat in front of the door and removed their mittens.

"Is there anything else we need while we're here?"

Althea glanced around. "Well, if you need soap or shampoo or hair spray," she teased. "This is the place to get it."

They ambled up and down the aisles grabbing a few items like aspirin and foot powder.

Clark shook his head. "I only ever shop at the grocery store. I'd forgotten there's a whole world of products out here."

She laughed. "You really need to get out more."

The bell above the main door tinkled as another customer arrived. Clark picked up Q-tips and tossed them into the basket Jack had retrieved.

He turned away from the shelf with a smile, but his smile suddenly froze and he stopped.

Confused, Althea followed his gaze to the tall dark-haired man who had just entered.

"Hey, Clark."

Clark stiffened. "Brice."

Brice? Althea's eyebrows rose. *The Brice?*

Her gaze flew to Clark. His face had hardened. His eyes had narrowed. His arms protectively hugged Teagan to him.

Teagan.

She hadn't worn a hat because she wanted everyone to see the red clip in her dark brown hair—hair the exact color of Brice's. She glanced at her eyes. Not whiskey-colored like Clark's but dark brown like Brice's.

She stifled a groan.

No wonder Clark worried. Teagan had Brice's coloring.

Thick, icy tension filled the space around them. Clark said nothing. Brice said nothing.

"We're just here for a few things," Althea said, putting her hands on Jack's shoulders and pulling him close to her. "So we need to get going."

Brice nodded. He nudged his head in the direction of the prescription counter. "I'm picking up something for my mom."

Not knowing what else to say, Althea said, "It was nice to see you," before she shepherded Clark and the kids away from him.

Clark didn't say a word on the drive home. Neither did Althea. What could she say? "I see why you're worried. Teagan looks just like him"?

He might need to talk about it, but that seemed a cruel way to bring up the subject. And they certainly wouldn't talk about it in front of the kids.

When they got home, he locked himself away in his office. Althea entertained Teagan and Jack. At six, she reheated the leftovers from their dinner the night before. But when she knocked on his office door, Clark said he wasn't hungry.

He did come out two hours later to help get Teagan ready for bed.

When she was bathed and in her pink princess pajamas, he read her the story about the bunny that had gotten lost in the woods. In the end of the book, when the daddy rabbit found the lost bunny, fed her soup, tucked her into bed and kissed her forehead telling her he'd never let anything happen to her, Teagan nestled into her pillow. Comforted. Happy.

She could always depend on her daddy.

With the story complete, Teagan's pink bedroom grew quiet. Clark rose, tucked her into the covers, kissed her forehead and said, "I'll never let anything happen to you." He kissed her forehead again. "You can always depend on me."

Teagan smiled. Her eyelids lowered.

Althea's eyes filled with tears. Teagan's favorite story wasn't just a story that comforted her. It comforted Clark, too.

As he passed the mirrored dresser, he picked up Teagan's hairbrush.

He stepped out of the room and closed the door.

She caught his gaze.

He sighed. "There's enough hair in here that the lab I found should be able to get something usable for a DNA sample."

Her breathing stilled. "I thought you'd already done that."

He shook his head. "I was a little preoccupied." He flicked his gaze to her again. "Happy."

"Oh." She swallowed. Grasping for something

to say, she said the first thing that popped into her head. "So how'd you get Brice's DNA?"

"I didn't. I don't want to know if she's his. I'm going to find out if she's mine. I'm sending my DNA."

He wouldn't look at her. A wall of distance sat between them.

She licked her dry lips. "And what's going to happen if it comes back she isn't your daughter?"

He shrugged. "Haven't figured that out yet." He sucked in a breath. "But after seeing him today, happy or not, able to pretend or not, I realized I can't put this off anymore. I have to know."

Without another word, he walked down the hall toward his bedroom. His shoulders hunched over, his steps slow, he looked like a man on his way to the gallows.

Sympathy overwhelmed her. His wife had been the one to make the mistakes, but he was the one suffering.

The mood the next morning was agonizing. Familiar silence permeated the room. She saw the package on Clark's briefcase, noticed the lab name neatly printed on the front.

Their gazes met as she sat down at the island with her cup of coffee.

Breaking the unbearable quiet, she said, "So Jack's going to be taking the tests today to see if he's ready to move into the next semester."

Clark worked up a smile. "That's great. Good luck, buddy."

Confident in the way only a twelve-year-old can be, Jack shrugged. "I'm going to ace this."

Clark chuckled. "Good."

The kitchen fell silent. Teagan munched on toast, grinning at Althea when she looked her way. She watched Clark's gaze amble over to his little girl and watched pain skitter into his eyes.

Everything inside her felt for him. If she could, she would take his pain. He was such a good man that it didn't seem fair that he had to suffer. He was a good person, an honest person, something she'd longed for all her life.

She swallowed. She had longed for this her entire life. A family with a man who protected his kids. A man who knew how to love.

Whether it was convenient or not, difficult or not, she loved him and she would not let this break him.

* * *

Clark returned home from work as down as he left. Althea tried to cheer him up through dinner.

"Jack was done with his tests twenty minutes before the average time."

"That's great."

"I think he deserves a treat tonight."

Clark met her gaze over the dinner table. "A treat?"

"I was thinking we could decorate the tree."

Jack gasped. "It's too early."

"It's less than a week before Christmas Eve." She sent a hopeful look Clark's way. "Besides, it's not like there's a law against decorating trees early when everybody seems to need a boost."

Catching her meaning, Clark sucked in a breath. "I suppose we could."

"I pulled the tree decorations from the attic and left them in the hall by the door again. Why don't you go get them, Jack?"

Jack said, "All right," grabbed Teagan's hand and flew out of the kitchen.

"It's not right for anybody to be sad this close to Christmas."

Clark sniffed a laugh. "So mine's the mood you're trying to boost."

"Not trying." She smiled. "I will boost your mood. But this is good for the kids, too."

She heard the thump, thump, thump of the big box being dragged down the stairs and Clara Bell's "Woof! Woof!"

She jumped out of her seat. "I think I better go help him."

Clark motioned her down. "You finish your dinner. I'll help."

Understanding that he might want some private time with the kids, Althea stayed behind, lingered over her dinner and put the dishes into the dishwasher.

When she couldn't delay any longer, she walked into the living room where Clark sat on the floor, artificial tree limbs sorted out in a big circle around him. Jack stood over his shoulder. Teagan stooped beside him.

"So what's up?"

He sighed. "I've always hated this tree."

Jack's eyes widened. "You have?"

"Yes. Now it isn't just artificial. It's old and artificial. I think I'd like a real tree."

Althea peeked over at him. He shrugged. "If we're going to make this our best Christmas ever, we should have a good tree."

Understanding what he was doing, she nodded. "I think that's a great idea. Is there a tree farm around here?"

Clark rose from the floor. "There are probably ten tree farms around here. But the best one is about five miles east." He faced the kids. "Get your coats."

Driving to the tree farm, Clark said, "This will be our new tradition. Going out a few days before Christmas and picking our own tree."

Althea's entire body tingled with happiness. She'd never helped choose a tree. But, better than that, she knew this adventure was good for the kids, as well as Clark. "I love real trees."

The closer they got to the tree farms, the happier he seemed to be. Not only did the tree shopping seem to take his mind off the DNA samples he'd sent that morning, but also this was a family who needed some new traditions.

When they arrived at the tree farm, Clark climbed out and helped Teagan out of her car seat. Carrying her, he walked to the makeshift stand in front of what looked like hundreds of rows of trees lit by huge overhead lights.

"We're here for a tree."

The old man running the stand pointed to the right where dozens of trees leaned against the side of an old building. "We have some pre-cut here or you can pick your own."

He glanced at the trees then Teagan's eager face. "I think I'd like the kids to have the experience of picking our own tree."

Her heart splintered in two for him and she suddenly understood. As he was putting together the artificial tree, he must have realized this might be his last Christmas with his little girl. And he intended to make it the best Christmas possible.

With Clark and Teagan leading the way, they started down one of the rows of trees. The music being piped around the farm shifted from "Here Comes Santa Claus" to "We Wish You a Merry Christmas." A light, powdery snow began to fall. Clark stopped in front of a tree.

"Look at this one."

She had to crane her neck to see the top. "I think it might be a bit too tall."

He nodded and started down the row again.

Teagan turned in her dad's arms and grinned at Althea who laughed. "We Wish You a Merry Christmas" floated around them. Caught in the spirit, Althea began to sing, too.

"We wish you a Merry Christmas. We wish you a Merry Christmas. We wish you a Merry Christmas and a Happy New Year."

"Glad tidings we bring to you and your kin." Jack joined in. Althea laughed and put her hand across his shoulder.

"We wish you a Merry Christmas," Clark joined in. "And a Happy New Year."

He stopped. "Hey, look at this one."

Althea and Jack stopped. The tree was tall, but not too tall. Bushy branches and a bright green color indicated a healthy tree.

"I think it's perfect."

"I think it's perfect, too." Clark looked to Jack. "What do you think?"

"I think it's great."

His voice was hushed, solemn, as if it was his first Christmas. In truth, it might actually be his first real Christmas since his mom's death.

Althea rubbed her hand across the top of his shoulders. "Wait until we get it decorated. I found so many beautiful ornaments in the boxes in the attic."

Jack nodded. "Should I go get the guy with the axe?"

Clark laughed. "I think a saw will be enough."

The caretaker sent one of his employees back with Jack to help cut the tree. He wrapped twine around the branches to make it possible to tie it to the top of the SUV. They were quiet on the way home, so Althea turned to face Teagan and Jack and began to sing, "We wish you a Merry Christmas."

Because that seemed to be the only song both she and Jack knew all the words for, they repeated it until Clark pulled in the driveway.

Shutting off the SUV engine he said, "Okay. Enough!" But he laughed. Jack laughed. Teagan giggled and Althea's spirits lifted. The dark cloud that seemed to have been hovering over Clark's head was gone. His eyes glowed with happiness as he and Jack wrestled the tree into the house.

Teagan stayed at Althea's side, her little mittened hand tucked firmly in Althea's.

And for the first time in her life she felt that she belonged. Not as a teacher or friend, but as someone more. Someone special not just to Clark, but to the kids, too.

Familiar fear tiptoed through her. Right now, making a Merry Christmas for the kids, she was good. Knowledgeable. All she had to do was figure out what *she* wanted, and do that for the kids. But what happened in January or February? What happened when they fell? Had a problem with a bully? This wasn't like school where she had a principal for backup or parents to call in for a consultation. She would be on her own and she had no idea how to handle kid troubles.

Jack and Clark installed the tree in the stand, then filled the bowl with water. Jack immediately walked over to the box of lights, but Clark stopped him. "It's late. Plus, we've had enough fun for tonight. Let's save some for tomorrow."

Jack looked about to argue but Althea said, "Tomorrow we can string popcorn and we'll have that to hang on the tree, too."

He said, "Okay."

"Great." Clark scooped up Teagan. "You guys can go find something on TV while I get Chai Tea ready for bed."

Jack headed for the den with Althea on his

heels. But she remembered she'd washed Teagan's favorite nightie that day. The fear nudged at her again. She'd forgotten laundry. Left it in the dryer like a single woman did. Not a mom. Not someone responsible for kids.

Telling herself to stop thinking of her failings, she changed directions. She pulled the clothes out of the dryer and hastily folded them. Carrying the armload of Teagan's T-shirts and pajamas, she raced up the stairs and into Teagan's bedroom.

Clark rushed in behind her.

She displayed the pajamas. "I forgot I'd washed these today."

He showed her a bottle of bath gel. "I forgot we'd run out of this last night."

Their gazes caught. Her fear eased a bit. Even seasoned father Clark forgot things a time or two. It might have been last minute that each had remembered, but they had remembered. In some ways that actually made them more compatible.

She smiled.

He smiled.

"We wish you a Merry Christmas and a Happy New Bear."

At the sound of the sweet little voice, both Clark and Althea pivoted to face the bathroom.

Clark whispered, "She's singing."

Too stunned to speak, Althea nodded.

As Teagan repeated "We Wish You a Merry Christmas and a Happy New Bear" over and over again, Clark and Althea sneaked up to the bathroom door, which was open a crack. They peeked inside.

Naked, waiting to go into the tub, Teagan sang to her dirty pink bear.

"Is she singing to the bear? Wishing the bear would have a happy Christmas?"

Althea pressed her hand to her mouth to stifle a laugh. "I think she's singing about a happy new bear because she doesn't have any frame of reference for a year, but she does know what a bear is."

"Oh." He paused. His eyes softened with love. "Look how beautiful she is."

"And how happy. She loves you Clark. She'll always be your little girl."

He blew his breath out on a long sigh. "Let's not kid ourselves, if the DNA tests come back that she's not my daughter chances are Brice will figure it out himself sooner or later."

"Maybe not."

"And what am I supposed to do if he doesn't? Keep her from her biological dad?"

She didn't know what to say, so she said nothing. Clark was in a horrible catch-22.

He opened the door and walked inside. Picking up Teagan, he tickled her tummy then put her in the tub. "We heard you singing."

She blushed and pressed her lips together.

Althea sat on the rim of the tub and ran her hand down Teagan's silky hair. "Oh, sweetie. You have such a beautiful voice. We loved hearing it."

She shook her head and looked down at the bubbly water around her.

She wasn't going to talk.

With a glance at Althea, Clark said, "Let's get you bathed and read your story."

Obviously relieved, Teagan nodded enthusiastically.

But walking down the stairs after Teagan was in bed, Clark sighed heavily. "You know that if a psychologist gets a hold of her and realizes she doesn't talk, only whispers, they'll crucify me.

They'll call me unfit and I'll never keep her. I'll be lucky to even get visitation rights."

Althea caught his arm. "That's if the DNA tests come back saying she's not yours. And if Brice sues you for custody. Don't borrow trouble."

He squeezed his eyes shut.

"Hey. Come on. I saw what you were doing tonight. You were working to make this the best Christmas ever. Don't stop now. Don't panic now. Keep going."

He hugged her. "Thank you."

She laughed. "For telling you not to borrow trouble? Or for bossing you around?"

"For being here. For making me face the truth. For not letting me get negative."

His arms tightened around her, and warmth filled her. She couldn't remember a time when somebody really wanted her around. Needed her. She might not be the best candidate for mom, but if Clark loved her she would make it work.

She prayed the DNA results came back saying Clark was Teagan's father.

Until then, she would keep this family happy.

CHAPTER ELEVEN

THE NEXT MORNING, she got up before Clark and had pancakes on the griddle when he entered the kitchen.

"What's that smell?"

She laughed. "It's breakfast. I worked the opening shift at the diner my last two years of high school. I make a mean pancake." And if she was going to do the job of keeping Clark and his kids happy while he awaited the DNA results, then she wasn't going to fudge or pretend. She wouldn't shy away from things she wanted to do, no matter how painful the memories. She would pull out all the stops—do everything she could do—to make these next few days happy.

"Mmmm." He sat on one of the stools around the center island as Teagan sleepily ambled into the room, bear under her arm.

Clark pointed at the stack of pancakes Althea walked to the table. "Look at those."

Her eyes rounded and she smiled.

"Teagan loves pancakes."

"Well, you are in luck," Althea said as she set the plate of pancakes on the center island and sat on the stool across from Clark. She picked up Teagan's plate. "How many do you want? Seven?"

She giggled.

Jack strolled into the room.

"Hey, buddy."

"Hey."

He slid onto a stool.

Clark pointed at the plate of pancakes. "Look. Althea made pancakes."

He roused himself a little. "Pancakes are good."

They passed syrup. Clark cut Teagan's pancake. Althea dug into her own.

"So what are you going to do today?"

Jack glanced up at his dad. "I don't know. What do you want me to do?"

"Well, you finished your studies so I guess you can choose."

"You mean if I want to play video games all day I can?"

"It's sort of like a vacation. You finished your work. You get the reward of time off."

He leaped off his stool. "Cool! I'm going to call Owen. See if he can play Wizard World with me online today."

Clark pointed at his plate. "First you have to eat."

He slid back onto the stool.

Clark gobbled his breakfast, grabbed his briefcase and headed for the door. As always, Althea followed him, giving him a chance to give her special instructions for the day if he had any.

Instead, he set down his briefcase, pulled her to him and kissed her. "I'll see you at dinnertime. Do you want me to bring home something?"

Too stunned to speak, she shook her head. He smiled. "Later."

She nodded.

He opened the door and closed it behind him.

She stared at it. Happiness swirled through her. One step at a time she could do this.

Midmorning, when Jack was in the den playing video games, Teagan sat coloring at the desk beside him and Althea studied a cookbook, looking for something special for dinner, the doorbell rang.

She jumped off the stool, calling, "I'll get it," as she passed the hall to the den.

Without thought, she grabbed the doorknob and yanked open the door with a festive, "Happy holidays."

"Well, happy holidays to you, too, baby girl."

Her dad.

Her chest froze as her gaze whipped around. The kids weren't behind her. She prayed they stayed in the den then pivoted to face her dad again.

"Get out."

"Hell, I'm not even in. I'm on the damned porch." He smiled at her. His gray whiskers lifting as his jowls rose. His beady eyes crinkling at the corners. "Besides, is that any way to treat your dad?"

"You were never a dad to me."

"Ah, hell, kitten. I did the best I could with what I had."

She gaped at him. "You had a successful business, a beautiful wife, two daughters who worked like slaves for you. And you rewarded us by beating us. You're a criminal."

He sniffed a laugh. "That's fancy talk from somebody who stole her daddy's car."

She shut up. Fear shivered through her. She recognized that voice. The warning voice. Hide before you get hit.

"In fact, that's pretty much why I'm here. I want blue book value on that car. Not what it's worth now. What it was worth the day you took it."

Her chin lifted. "You never paid us for working at the diner. I think of taking that car as evening the scales."

"State police don't see it that way. I ran a hypothetical past them and they say I'm entitled to restitution…or I can have you locked up."

Her heart stuttered. She automatically took a pace back. He could be lying. He always lied. But this wasn't something to test him on. Eventually, she intended to pay him, but she couldn't today. Not only was her bank account empty, but she also hadn't printed out the receipt and release form she'd found at the legal site online. Plus, if she told him she would pay him later, he'd hound her to borrow the money or give him a post-dated check—or something. And then he'd be back because she didn't yet have a release for him to sign.

"I don't have any money."

He peered into the foyer. "Seems like your boyfriend does."

"He's not my boyfriend. I'm his son's teacher."

"So what do you get for this gig? Has to be good. More than a teacher's salary."

Her heart stumbled again.

He pointed his index finger at her nose. "I'll be back after the holidays. You have my money for me then."

He smiled, turned and walked away.

She closed the door behind him then leaned against it. Her knees shook so much it was everything she could do not to slide down to the floor and wrap herself in a tight ball. Hot, prickly fear enveloped her. But it wasn't fear for herself. It was fear for Teagan, Jack and even Clark.

This was why she couldn't have a relationship. Anybody she brought into her life would have to deal with her dad.

When Clark arrived in his office, he had thirty-seven emails waiting. But he saw only one that concerned him. Jack's test scores.

He blew his breath out on a sigh and prayed the

results were good because Jack was counting on this. Althea was right. He needed to go to school in town, needed friends. But if he failed and had to enter school a grade below his peers that might be worse than not going to school at all.

Slowly, deliberately, he clicked on the email and the message popped up on his screen. As he read the scores, his frown lifted into a grin. Jack had done it!

He sat back on his chair. *Althea* had done it. She'd worked real magic on his family.

He called the house to see if she'd be free to go to the school with him that afternoon but got no answer. Realizing she might have taken the kids Christmas shopping, he chuckled…then stopped himself. *He'd chuckled.* He really wasn't afraid anymore. Wasn't dead inside. She'd brought him back to life.

He called the school and set an appointment to meet with the principal that afternoon. He tried the house again, but again got no response, so he went to the redbrick school alone.

He sat in the office, in a chair meant to accommodate a middle-school kid, feeling tall and

gangly. He jumped out of his seat when Mrs. Osborne stepped out of her office.

"Mr. Beaumont?"

"Yes." He extended his hand to shake hers. "I'd
like to enroll my son for the next semester."

"That's wonderful." She directed him to go into
her office. "I trust you have his transcripts."

The first ten minutes Clark took care of the
business of transcripts and qualifications, then he
sucked in a breath and did what had to be done.

"Jack's mom was killed in an automobile accident three years ago."

Mrs. Osborne laid her arms on her desk. "I remember."

"There was gossip."

She winced. "I remember that, too."

"I'm afraid it will resurrect when he returns
to school."

"It might. But the interesting thing about middle school is that the kids don't really care so
much what their parents do. They're quite self-
absorbed."

He laughed. "For once that would work in my
favor." But he quickly sobered. If the DNA test
results came back that Teagan wasn't his, he had

some big decisions to make and those decisions could impact Jack.

He sucked in another breath. He didn't want to tell his secrets, his shame, to a complete stranger, but he did want Jack to be protected.

"Just in case these kids aren't so self-absorbed, how about if you have Jack's teacher report anything unusual to you."

She brought her hands together and knitted her fingers. "Define unusual."

"You know…if he's bullied, teased, that kind of thing."

"We're very proud of our antibullying policies. We will protect your son. But, it's also our policy to alert parents if there's any extra trouble."

He nodded. Rose. He couldn't ask for anything more than to be apprised. But he still had a sense he was leading his son into a den of lions and it sickened him, resurrected his anger with his dead wife, made him feel powerless.

Never in his life had anyone been able to make him feel powerless…until Carol.

When Clark arrived home, Althea could see he was antsy, nervous. Their moods fit and she was glad. With him upset, it was unlikely he'd notice she was upset.

She'd intended to make something fancy and festive for supper and instead only had the mental energy to open two cans of soup and make cheese sandwiches.

Teagan loved it. Jack ate three sandwiches. Clark barely touched his food.

When the kids disappeared before having to stack the dishes in the dishwasher, Clark sniffed a laugh. "Well, we sort of made our bed on that one."

A shiver raced through her at his unexpected choice of words. "Our bed?"

He met her gaze. "Neither one of us talked enough to slow down the kids' eating and keep them here long enough to do dishes."

She almost laughed at the silly way she'd misinterpreted him, but nerves overwhelmed her. If she wanted to have a life with Clark, she didn't just have to tell him about her dad's visit. She had to admit her dad had found her. Wanted money. Would probably want more money, even after she paid for the car.

"I visited Jack's school today."

"Oh." Good news. Thank God. She could certainly use it.

"I got his grades this morning." He shook his head. "Damn. I should have printed them out and shown him."

Althea smiled. "He knows he did well. He'll be okay waiting another day or two to actually see his scores."

"He did exceptionally well." He reached across the table and squeezed her hand. "Thanks to you."

Her spirits lifted a bit. "You're welcome."

"Anyway, I enrolled him for the next semester."

"That's great." Her spirits rose again.

"It seems great." He toyed with his silverware. "I just hope I'm not throwing him to the lions."

"Sixth-graders are bad, but they're not lions."

He met her gaze. "No, but their parents are. What the hell is going to happen if I get the DNA results back and Teagan's not mine? What if Brice picks this year to finally figure out she might be his? What if I decide Teagan has a right to know her real dad?" He squeezed his eyes shut. "Is this the right year to put him into school?"

"I don't know."

He burst from his stool. "Damn it all, anyway! What the hell was Carol thinking? How could she bring this trouble to our door? Where the hell was her head?"

She swallowed. "I don't know."

He raked his fingers through his hair. "I can't even comprehend that level of selfishness."

Althea stayed quiet. She might not have betrayed Clark the way his deceased wife had, but if she stayed, she'd bring every bit as much trouble to his house.

He shook his head as if shaking off his anger and faced her. "I'll do the dishes."

She rose. "No. I'll do the dishes. You need to get the kids and start decorating the tree we bought yesterday."

"That's right."

She smiled. "I know you want to make this a special holiday for the kids and I think having something to do every night like decorating the tree is an excellent way to do that. Don't let the past ruin the present."

He nodded. "You're right. How'd you get so smart?"

She looked away. "Oh, I am so far away from

smart that you'd be amazed." She tossed a dish-towel at him. "Go or I'll make you dry."

He started out of the room, but stopped suddenly. "There's one more thing."

"Oh, yeah?"

"All this time you've been here, I've never paid you."

She tilted her head. "No. You haven't."

"So, I transferred your salary into the checking account number you gave me."

A thrill of happiness ran through her. She'd loved working here, even without pay. But that money had a purpose. It gave her choices rather than have to become a baker by default.

"I also added a bonus."

"Oh, Clark! You shouldn't have done that!"

"Hey, you washed dishes, did laundry, baby-sat the kids…all things that weren't in the job description when I hired you. You earned the money."

Grateful, she smiled. "Thanks."

He left the room and Althea made short order of the dishes. Her mood improved, she raced into her room and fired up her laptop. In a few quick keystrokes, she was at her banking account page and when she saw the amount Clark had deposited, her eyes bulged. Over double what they'd agreed to.

She rose, ready to go into the living room and argue, except…

It was enough money to pay off her dad.

She paced her room. The problem was no amount was ever enough money to pay off her dad. Still, if she gave him this money she needed documentation that she'd paid off the car. That their debt was settled. Before she gave him a check, she had to print out the receipt and release she'd found on the legal website, stating that her debt to him was paid in full.

But that wouldn't stop him from asking again.

And again.

And again.

Missy had told her that.

She'd told her that the only way to get rid of him was to stand up to him. And she wasn't sure she could. Oh, she would try. She would go to him with the best of intentions, but he'd baby girl her…or he'd threaten her and her knees would knock together.

She stopped pacing. She'd never been able to

face him for herself, but for Clark, Teagan and Jack...

Her shoulders straightened. For Clark, Teagan and Jack, she could pay him his money, get him to sign the receipt and tell him she would call the police if he ever came near her again. That's what Missy had done. It would work for her, too.

She closed her laptop and headed into the living room. Clark and Jack had strung multicolored lights in rows on the tree. Teagan walked a shiny red ornament to one of the bottom branches and hung it.

Jack saw her first. "You missed all the cursing."

She laughed. "Lights that hard to string?"

"No. They were tangled. Right, Dad?"

"Tangled doesn't even begin to describe it."

They had two more days until Christmas Eve. The house was decorated. The tree was being decorated. They could bake cookies the next day or she and Jack could do a special project.

"I was thinking." She bit her lip. "We don't really have any more decorating to do tomorrow. We could bake cookies—"

Jack fist-pumped. "All right!"

"Or we could take the family pictures off your

dad's computer and send them to a photo site. When the pictures get here next week, we could create photo albums." She paused, caught Clark's gaze. "We could make special albums for you and Teagan," she said, still talking to Jack, though she looked to Clark for approval. "Albums with memories of your mom."

Jack said, "That would be nice."

Clark smiled. "That would be really nice."

They finished decorating the tree. Clark thought of another memory or two to tell his kids. Althea's nerves calmed. She would face her dad as soon as she could sneak away. Not for herself but to protect the new family she was creating.

She was so high on happiness that she began singing "We Wish You a Merry Christmas." Jack joined in immediately. Clark soon after. Teagan grinned.

Althea stooped in front of her. "We know you know this."

The little girl giggled.

Clark said, "Yeah, Teagan. We know you know this song."

She giggled again.

"One of these days you're going to forget your-self and talk to us."

She laughed and hugged her bear to her face.

But that night when Althea went upstairs to put away some of Jack's laundry, she heard Teagan singing in the bathroom again and she smiled. Clark was right. One of these days his little girl would relax enough and be calm enough to for-get she didn't talk out loud and she'd just speak.

She walked down the stairs feeling light and airy. Everything was working out. Once she got rid of her dad all she had to do was take life one day at a time.

She could do this.

But when she walked into the den, Clark wasn't in front of the TV. He paced back and forth be-hind the desk.

"What's up?"

"In all the commotion of getting Jack into school again, I forgot I was supposed to get the DNA results today."

"So soon?"

"I paid extra to have the tests expedited."

"So, check your computer now."

He faced her. "I just did. They aren't there. So much for the extra money I paid."

She plopped to the sofa. "Come on. Sit down. Watch some TV. Worrying's not going to accomplish anything."

He sat. "I just want to know."

"No matter what happens, you are her father. Even if Brice gets custody, the judge would let you have visitation. You'll never really lose her. Your role would just change."

"I wouldn't like that."

"No. But it would be better than nothing. But I don't think you're going to lose custody. I actually think it might flip. You'd keep custody and Brice would get visitation. You've raised her. You're the only father she knows. No judge would pull her away from you."

"You don't think so?"

"I think you have to focus on the positive options. Not the negative. And that includes remembering that she could actually be your daughter."

He sniffed a laugh. "I tell myself that a few times a day now." He caught her gaze. "You came into my life at just the right moment. Jack needed you. But I needed you more. I needed someone to kick my butt and tell me it was time to move on. I appreciate everything you've done."

She smiled, waiting for more. Telling her he appreciated everything she'd done was a perfect opportunity for him to tell her that he loved her. Or that he wanted her. Or even something as simple as he liked her. But he said nothing. He turned to the TV.

She glanced at the TV, then back at him. He wasn't the only one who had a problem. Now that she knew how she wanted to handle her dad, she could talk to him about it. She needed the same support from him that she gave to him. She wanted to share her troubles, her dreams… her life. She wanted him to love her.

And he was watching TV.

Of course, he'd had a stressful day, made worse by the fact that the DNA test results hadn't come as they were supposed to.

She slid close to him on the sofa. He put his arm around her. And though she didn't nestle in, she relaxed.

Everything was fine.

But at eleven, when he excused himself to go to bed he didn't even think to kiss her.

She watched him leave the room, reminding herself he'd had a rough day. Hell, he'd had a rough three years that was about to culminate in either the best or worst news of his life. She couldn't fault him for being preoccupied.

The next morning she rose early again. Not only did she need to prove to herself that she could fit into this family, but also she'd promised herself she'd do whatever it took to keep them happy.

She made oatmeal—every day couldn't be a pancake celebration day—and though Jack groaned, Teagan clapped with glee. Clark also entered the kitchen looking bright and chipper.

Scooping a bowl of oatmeal for himself, he said, "Remember the email I told you I was waiting for?"

Her breath froze and she spun to face him. There was only one piece of news he had been waiting for.

"It turns out I had been worrying for nothing. The last project Carol had been working on belongs to me."

Joy burst inside her. She wanted to run to him and hug him. News like this deserved fanfare…

a celebration. But he'd used code so he could tell her without letting the kids in on a secret they were too young to know. She couldn't hug him.

Of course, if they were going to have a relationship, why delay letting the kids see? Why not hug him? Wasn't that what a normal person would do?

She peered over at him. He dished oatmeal into a bowl.

She couldn't hug a man holding a bowl of oatmeal. So she smiled. "That's great."

"Yeah, Dad, I hope you get the bid."

Clark ruffled Jack's hair. "The wait is over. It's mine."

Althea chuckled at the double meaning in that and joined them at the breakfast table.

Clark said, "So today's the day you look through pictures on the computer?"

"I thought we'd do that in the morning and bake cookies in the afternoon."

Teagan gasped and clapped before she slid off her stool, ran to Clark and tugged on his shirt-sleeve.

Clark shook his head and kissed the top of her

head. "Nope. No more whispering. I want you to talk."

She frowned. Althea's eyebrows rose. With the worry of her paternity issues out of the way, Clark wasn't going so easy on her. She frowned and sulked her way back to her stool.

Clark ate his oatmeal reading the *Wall Street Journal,* then left for work. He didn't catch her shoulders, pull her to him and give her a quick kiss. He didn't smile at her. Actually, he was so caught up in gathering his briefcase and coat that he barely looked at her.

This time she couldn't blame it on him being preoccupied. Jack's grades were up. The DNA results were in. Now that he was free of worry and happy, he seemed to have forgotten all about her.

She shook that off. Told herself that was ridiculous. But actions spoke louder than words. He hadn't noticed her worry the day before. He'd hardly noticed her that morning.

She occupied herself helping the kids choose the pictures for the albums in the morning. But she couldn't stop the worry over his indifference that morning. To take her mind off that, she and the kids made cookies all afternoon.

When Clark returned from the office, the house was filled with the scent of sugar and cinnamon, as well as the roasted chicken, mashed potatoes and peas she'd made for dinner.

He scooped Teagan up on his way to the kitchen. When she was seated at the table, he pulled a piece of paper out of his jacket pocket and handed it to Jack.

He opened it and jumped for joy. "I knew I'd done well."

Feeling oddly left out, Althea said, "Oh, so those are your grades?"

He nodded. "Here. See for yourself. I did excellently."

Reading the report, she smiled. "I'm very proud of you."

Clark said, "I'm very proud of you, too."

They ate dinner companionably chatting about Jack's grades and his reentry into "real" school.

When they were through, Clark stole a cookie for dessert. "Jack, how about putting these dishes in the dishwasher?"

Still excited over his good grades, he happily jumped off his chair. "Sure."

Clark caught Althea's hand. "I thought you and I could have a private minute in the garage."

"The garage?" Good Lord. All day she'd worried that he didn't want anything to do with her anymore and here he was spiriting her out to the garage to kiss her. Her happiness returned in a wave of joy. She was such a worrywart!

He put his finger over his lips and made a shhh sound as he led her down the hall to the door that would take them to the garage. "I went to the mall today. And I think I got the doll Teagan wanted. I need you to look at it to be sure."

"Oh." She wasn't exactly disappointed. She wanted Teagan to have that special doll as much as he did, but for the past few days their communication had been all about the kids. About him. And then this morning he'd all but ignored her. Though he'd said he appreciated her the night before, the spark of whatever he'd felt for her seemed to be gone.

In the garage, he took the doll out of a huge bag of things he'd bought for the kids. All her odd feelings disappeared. He was getting ready for Christmas…for his kids. He might not be preoccupied with Jack's grades or Teagan's DNA, but now Christmas was on his mind. How could she fault him for that?

She smiled at him. "This is the doll."

"Damn, I'm good."

She laughed. "Yes, you are."

Suddenly, Jack appeared at the door. "Hey, Dad! Mrs. Alwine's here!"

He grabbed the doll from Althea's hands and tossed it back into his SUV before racing to the door.

Althea followed him.

A tall, thin woman stood in the kitchen, holding Teagan, who hugged her fiercely as if she'd never let her go.

Clark raced over. "Mrs. Alwine! It's so good to see you! How are you feeling?"

"I'm great. You were right. The extra week of recovery time worked wonders."

He was right? He'd spoken to Mrs. Alwine and never told her?

"That's great."

Mrs. Alwine laughed. "Yeah. It's great. But I know you need someone to cook for your holiday and I'm back."

Althea watched as Jack slid on a stool and Clark

chatted happily about how they'd gotten on without her because of Althea.

"That's good. Jack's grades are up then?"

Clark said, "Yes."

He talked to her almost the same way he'd spoken to Althea. Friendly. Inclusive. Mrs. Alwine
knew as much about Jack as Althea had. With
her here, it was as if Althea had no place. Worse,
she wasn't the fifty-year-old woman Althea had
pictured her to be. She was probably thirty-five.
Young. Happy. Energetic. She probably made
cookies. Made supper. Remembered the laundry. And Teagan loved her. So did Jack. So did
Clark. Not in the romantic way she'd thought he
felt about her. But he clearly loved seeing her,
having her back.

"So I can be here tomorrow morning." She tickled Teagan's tummy. "We can bake cookies."

Teagan laughed.

"We made cookies." And didn't she feel like
an idiot for pointing it out.

Mrs. Alwine smiled. "What did you make?"

"Snicker doodles and shaped sugar cookies.
We painted them."

She tickled Teagan's tummy again. "Then we'll make chocolate chip."

Jack said, "All right!"

Clark smiled.

And Althea suddenly wondered if she hadn't misinterpreted everything.

Was she so desperate for love that she read things into everything Clark said that he didn't really mean?

CHAPTER TWELVE

Mrs. Alwine left with a promise to return in the morning. Althea was on her way to her room, when Clark said, "Hey, why don't we make hot cocoa and sit in front of the tree?"

The kids cheered, so Althea headed for the cupboard with the pans. Jack pulled the cocoa and sugar from the pantry. Clark got the milk. Teagan sat on a tall stool by the center island, her elbow on the marble island top and her chin on her closed fist.

They took the tray of four cups of cocoa into the living room, and Clark turned on the tree lights. Teagan gasped. Jack settled on the cushiony area rug beneath the coffee table. Clark and Althea sat on the sofa.

Clark said, "Do we want to sing?"

Teagan shook her head fiercely. Althea laughed. "We're not trying to bamboozle you into talking out loud. Singing is part of the holidays."

She shook her head again.

Jack rose unexpectedly. "Yeah. You know what? I'm kinda tired, too."

Althea's gaze whipped to Teagan who all but drooped at the coffee table. "Oh." She'd been so wrapped up in herself and Clark that she hadn't noticed. She rose. "Well, let's put Teagan to bed then."

Clark waved her down. "I'll get this. You take a break. You've been busy all day."

When Clark and the kids were gone, she leaned back on the sofa, telling herself to calm down. But she couldn't.

Part of her worried that she didn't fit into this household as well as she'd believed. The other part was worried sick about her dad. In her head, she knew the two things were connected. That if she could talk about her dad with Clark then she would relax, stop noticing stupid things and fit again.

She sucked in a breath, staring at the pretty tree. As Clark had mentioned a time or two, Carol had had excellent taste. Though the tree had no theme, the pristine multicolored balls and bells were uniform in size. The multicolored lights shimmered. Silver tinsel bowed from limb to limb leading to the angel who sat on top, like a guardian.

Clark strolled into the room. "Well, that's done for the night."

Althea nervously picked up her cocoa.

Clark plopped down beside her. "You look tired yourself."

"I am. And I—" She faltered. Though it hadn't seemed difficult to tell him the story of her past, she couldn't seem to find the words to tell him her dad was very much in her present. Every time she opened her mouth, she remembered him angry with Carol, wondering what she'd been thinking, bringing this much trouble to their door, and the words choked back. Logically, Carol hadn't thought she'd die. She hadn't known Teagan's paternity would be called into question. She hadn't thought her affair would become public.

Althea, on the other hand, knew her dad, knew he wanted money.

Clark scooted over, slid his hand across her shoulders.

She jumped, then winced. "Sorry."

He leaned in and kissed her. "Don't be sorry.

I just realized how preoccupied I'd been." He smiled. "I hoped I could make it up to you."

She wanted him to. With every fiber of her being she wanted him to. She brushed her lips across his lightly. "What'd you have in mind?"

He returned her kiss. "Oh, a little of this and a little of that."

She laughed. Her tension ebbed. She also remembered that she had a plan to handle her father. Maybe she shouldn't tell Clark until she'd taken care of it?

He slid closer, pushed her down on the sofa cushion and kissed her again. It felt like coming home. Until the last few days, being with Clark had always been easy. Then Jack's grades came back good and that problem was solved. DNA results showed Teagan was Clark's. Mrs. Alwine returned…and no one needed her.

She stopped that thought. Clark wouldn't be kissing her if he didn't need her. The oddness she suddenly felt wasn't from Clark. Ever since her dad had shown up she'd been suspicious, antsy, nervous.

Just as she had been when she'd lived with him. She knew she was going to take care of him, pay for the car, but she hadn't been able to tell Clark about her dad's visits—

She suddenly realized she wanted to talk. She needed to get this out. To share it. That was part of what being a couple was all about.

She stopped kissing him, angled up a bit so that he rose too.

"I…um…"

He gave her a hand to help her up. "It's all right." He smiled. "I don't want to force you into something you're not ready for."

"I might actually be ready. Except—"

He laughed. "I know. Everybody's tired. Jack fell asleep as soon as his head hit the pillow. Teagan didn't even hear her whole story. What'd you and the kids do today?" He shook his head with another laugh. "Whatever it was tomorrow will be better. With Mrs. Alwine here again, you don't have to worry about dinner or laundry or tidying up. And I'll be home all day." He kissed her again. A quick, smacking kiss.

"It's not that. My dad—"

He stopped her by putting his index finger over her lips. "Sweetie. This is our first holiday together. Don't spoil it for yourself by remembering things that will make you sad. Enjoy it."

She blinked, confusion and despair overwhelmed her. She was drowning and he didn't see. That was the real problem. She'd been there for him every step of the way, helping him handle his problem with Jack and Teagan, but now that she needed him, he wasn't hearing her.

Still, she might have been nervous and distracted, but he wasn't a mind reader. Though she'd told him about her dad in the past, she hadn't told him he'd shown up at their front door.

"It's just that he—"

He shook his head. "Althea, he's spoiled every Christmas for you from the time you were a baby. Get it out of your head!"

"He's *here*."

"What?"

"He came here the other day. He wants the money for the car."

"We'll give him the money for the car."

"It's not that easy."

He rose, extending his hand to her. "Come on. Go to bed. Get some sleep. In the morning, when you're not so tired, you'll see this isn't as terrible as you think it is."

She almost stomped her foot and demanded that he listen to her, but the very fact that she wanted to rant and rave made her wonder if he wasn't right. Maybe she was tired?

In her bedroom, she picked up her cell phone and saw a text from her dad.

Do you have my money yet?

She squeezed her eyes shut. She knew Clark was being supportive, but it wasn't enough. She wanted her dad gone. She didn't want to involve Clark and the kids. This family was finally healing, and if Clark got involved she would bring more trouble to their doorstep.

She barely slept that night, so the next morning she didn't find the relief Clark had assured her she would. Mrs. Alwine had breakfast made—bacon, eggs and toast. Clark stared at his computer screen while he ate his. Teagan grinned happily. Jack chattered about playing another online game with Owen.

When breakfast was done, she excused herself to her room, showered, put on clean jeans and a sweater. She walked through the kitchen, on her way to the den to find the kids, but the kids weren't in the den. She checked the living room with the tree and their bedroom and Clark's office.

Finding no one, she ambled back to the kitchen where Mrs. Alwine was leafing through a cookbook.

"Where is everybody?"

Mrs. Alwine laughed. "Special, private mission."

"Oh."

And they hadn't invited her. They hadn't even told her they were leaving.

Still, she smiled at Mrs. Alwine.

Clark and the kids returned an hour later. They'd had lunch at the mall, so when Althea suggested they all sit down to eat, they told her to eat without them and raced away.

She sat at the kitchen table alone, while Mrs. Alwine puttered around.

"We're making chocolate chip cookies this afternoon if you'd like to join us."

Althea glanced up. "Sure. That would be fun."

Mrs. Alwine brought her coffee to the table and

sat. "I know it always seems odd when people come and go mysteriously. But it is Christmas."

She smiled.

"And the kids must love making cookies with you because they've talked about it nonstop."

Althea nodded.

Mrs. Alwine shook a finger at her. "So don't be so blue."

She laughed and helped with the cookies that afternoon, but everything was different.

She was nervous about her dad, unsure about what was going on with her and Clark and now the kids were behaving oddly around her.

That night after the kids were in bed, eager for Christmas Eve the next day, Althea found Clark and confronted him.

"I get it that I'm not a member of the family. But you've told me things even you admitted you'd never told anyone else. So the only reason I can figure out that you and the kids left without telling me today is that you left because of something to do with me."

He sat back on his chair. Gave her a shuttered look. "It does."

Her heart deflated. Dear God. She was so sure

he was about to tell her she was paranoid that when he said their secret *was* about her she nearly collapsed.

"I see."

She turned to go but he caught her hand and yanked her to him so hard she fell to his lap. "Althea! It's Christmastime. The kids had me take them out to buy you gifts."

Embarrassment overwhelmed her. Oh, God.

He laughed. "They wanted it to be a surprise."

Tears filled her eyes. "I'm so sorry."

"You're tired! You're a single woman who spent an entire month being a mom to two troubled kids. Now that it's over you're decompressing or something."

He placed a smacking kiss on her lips, pushed her off his lap and smacked her bottom. "Go to bed."

She walked back to her room like a zombie. Her fears forgotten. Her suspicions obliterated. Her mind numb.

She'd felt left out when they were actually doing something nice for her.

She walked into her room, closed the door and leaned against it. It was like being fourteen again, suspecting her dad was mad at her, worried that he'd find out something she didn't want him to know.

She flopped to the bed, put her head in her hands. This wasn't about her dad. Clark and the kids weren't wrong to want to surprise her. They were sweet and she didn't know how to deal with sweet. Hell, she didn't know how to deal with normal.

The tears that had gathered in Clark's office spilled over. He thought she was tired. But she wasn't tired; she was ruined. She didn't know how to trust. She did her best work in problems. That's why she was so good, almost normal, when Jack had troubles and Clark was worried.

Now that they were normal, she floundered.

She swiped her hands across her cheeks to brush away the tears and felt their shaking.

She didn't deserve this family. She most certainly wouldn't put wonderful Clark through another bad relationship. Damn it! He'd suffered enough—three long years—because of Carol.

She would not put him through anything else.

Sobbing uncontrollably, she rose from the bed, retrieved her suitcase and began packing. Tomorrow was Christmas Eve so she wouldn't ruin the kids' Christmas. They had Mrs. Alwine. Clark was healed and whole and able to give them their best Christmas ever. But if she stayed and they gave her their gifts, she would crumble. She'd never be able to leave and Clark would be stuck with another woman who only gave him heartache.

With her clothes packed and her laptop strap over her shoulder, she sneaked through the dark downstairs. All the lights off meant Clark had already gone to bed. She breathed a sigh of relief. Not letting herself take one last longing look toward the upstairs or the Christmas tree twinkling in the moonlight pooling in through the big window, she reached for the doorknob.

"I want pigtails."

She froze, then spun around. "Teagan," she whispered. A laugh bubbled up. "I told you when you really wanted something you'd talk."

Teagan displayed two matching hair ties she held. "I want pigtails."

She set her suitcases on the floor, slid her laptop beside them. "Honey," she whispered. "You're supposed to be in bed."

Teagan's response was to shove the two hair ties at her.

She laughed. Rifling through her purse she found a comb. "Okay. We'll do this quickly."

She pulled the comb through Teagan's long dark locks, quickly parted it down the middle of the back of her head and spun the hair ties around two loose ponytails, one by each ear.

She smiled, turning Teagan to face her. "You look adorable."

Teagan grinned. "I know."

She shook her head. "So you're going to talk now?"

She nodded. And Althea felt the door closing on this chapter of her life. With Teagan talking everything that was wrong when she arrived had been fixed.

"Where are you going?"

"I'm just taking a little drive."

Teagan frowned. "I want you to stay."

Pain poured through her. She wanted to stay, too. More than anything she'd ever wanted. But she was broken. Ruined. And this family had just healed. She wouldn't put them through living with her doubts and insecurities.

She stooped in front of Teagan who stood on the third stair up. "I would like to stay, but I can't. I have to go see my sister." That was a bit of a lie, but not really. She'd see Missy before she left town.

Teagan looked down at the stair below her. "But I want you to stay here."

"Sometimes people can't stay. Sometimes people come into our lives when we need them, but they're only here to do a job then they leave."

She peeked up. "Like an angel."

She laughed. She'd hardly call herself an angel. Still, if it made Teagan happy... "Yes. Like an angel. Now go to bed."

Teagan nodded and turned to go up the stairs. But she stopped suddenly and came back down, propelling herself into Althea's arms. "I wub you."

Althea pressed her lips together. "I love you, too."

CHAPTER THIRTEEN

CLARK WOKE UP excited, happier than he'd been in years. It was Christmas Eve and he was in love. In *love.* Real love.

He'd known there was something different, something special about Althea from the day he interviewed her. But he never would have realized that trusting her would lead him to face his fears. And the reward was the freedom to love her.

He sleepily walked into the kitchen. Jack sat at the center island, eating a bowl of cereal and reading a book.

A book.

Dear God. Could that woman have had any more of a positive impact on them? He'd said he didn't deserve her and maybe he didn't. But he would spend the rest of his life loving her.

He glanced longingly down the hall. Her door was closed, which meant she was still sleeping.

"We should do something special for Althea."

Jack looked up. "Like what? We already got her a gift."

"I know, but maybe we should go out to dinner tonight?"

Even as the words came out of his mouth they felt wrong. What was he doing inviting Jack and Teagan out on his first date with Althea? He couldn't leave the kids with a sitter on Christmas Eve, but the day after Christmas he intended to take her out. Someplace special.

Mrs. Alwine burst into the room from the garage entry. Unwrapping her scarf, she said, "What are you two doing up at six?"

Jack said, "I was hungry."

Clark laughed. "I thought it was later."

"It's still dark out!" She cast a quick glance at Jack's cereal. "I was going to make apple pancakes."

Jack shoved his bowl away. "Make 'em."

Clark sat beside Jack as Teagan walked into the room, rubbing her eyes. "Hey, pumpkin."

Her hair in cockeyed pigtails, which, given their sloppiness, she'd probably done herself, she frowned and walked over to him. He lifted her into his lap. "It's Christmas Eve! Little girls aren't supposed to be grouchy on Christmas Eve. Althea's gonna be mad at you."

"No, she's not."

Clark froze. Jack's head snapped up. Mrs. Alwine faced them with a gasp.

"Teagan! You talked."

Jack high-fived her. "Way to go, Chai Tea."

Teagan snuggled into her dad's shirt. "She doesn't wuv us. She said she does but she doesn't."

The sadness in her voice finally penetrated. "What? Are you talking about Althea?"

She nodded.

"Don't be silly. She adores you."

"She weft."

The joy of hearing Teagan speak was quickly shoved aside by paralyzing fear. "What?" It was early. Way too early for Althea to have gone to the store. Plus, Teagan had just gotten up. How could she say Althea had left?

"Did you have a bad dream?"

She shook her head. Her cockeyed pigtails swung from side to side.

Clark bounced her once on his lap. "Come on, now. You're talking. You're not going back to nods and frowns. Tell Daddy. Did you have a bad dream?"

"She made my pigtails then told me she had to weave."

Clark froze. Took another look at the pigtails. Especially, the tightness of the brightly colored hair ties. They weren't the handiwork of a three-year-old. They'd gone cockeyed from Teagan sleeping on them.

He spun her around on his lap. "She left last night?"

Teagan nodded.

"Did she have her suitcases?"

She nodded again.

Clark's heart fell to his feet. He plopped Teagan on the stool beside Jack and raced to her room.

Neat as a pin, the bed had been made. The drapes drawn. The closet emptied. He spun to the dresser and saw the note leaning against the mirror.

He grabbed it and ripped it open.

"I'm sorry to leave like this. But with Jack's studies completed and Mrs. Alwine back I realized I could go. My dad wants restitution for the car and thanks to you I can give it to him. But he's a royal pain in the butt and if I stay, he'll always hound us. I'll never forget you guys."

He threw the note on the bed, raised his gaze to the ceiling. He'd felt she was a little nervous the past few days, but he thought that was because everything was happening between them. So he'd given her space, distance, to work out how she was feeling.

"Do you wuv her, Daddy?"

He spun to face Teagan. Mrs. Alwine raced behind her and put her hands on Teagan's little shoulders. "I'll just take her to the kitchen and let her help me make pancakes."

She turned Teagan to go as Clark stared around the room feeling something akin to despair. She was worried about them. He got that. He could handle her dad. But he sensed she didn't want him to.

Confused, disheartened, he returned to the kitchen.

At the center island Teagan was crying. "I want Alfeea."

He slumped on the stool beside her. "I want Althea, too." His brain scrambled for answers. What had he done? Why had he decided to give her time and distance? He should have pushed her. He should have let her know what she meant to them.

But, no. He'd had to be logical. And now he'd lost her.

Althea walked down the dark, silent Main Street of Newland. Cold air turned her breath to mist as she strode purposefully to the diner. She stopped at the door and squeezed her eyes shut, but popped them open again. This was something she had to do.

Then she could go. Away from Missy. Away from Clark. Away so that people with normal lives didn't have to be hurt.

She pushed open the door and the bell sounded. The sweet scent of cinnamon rolls filled the air. Empty booths and tables sat silently in the semi-dark dining room. Christmas Eve. People would pour in for fresh cinnamon rolls around nine. Until then, he'd be alone.

"Gimme a minute, early bird," he called from

the kitchen. When it came to his customers, he was Mr. Personality. That's how she and Missy had known no one would believe them if they sought help. Who would possibly believe such a great guy, a solid business owner, hurt his wife and daughters?

He walked out of the kitchen wiping his hands on a dishtowel. When he saw her he stopped and smiled. "Well, hey, baby girl. Merry Christmas."

The nickname went through her like a knife. She crushed the check in her pocket. Fear trembled through her, but she remembered that the check in her sweaty hand meant freedom. She took two steps to the counter.

"So what do you want? Free pancakes? A dozen cinnamon rolls to impress your boyfriend?" He snorted a laugh. "Ain't nothing comes free in this life. You pay like everybody else."

"I paid more than everybody else."

His face scrunched in contempt. "Excuse me?"

"What are you going to do? Hit me?"

Before he could reply, she slapped the check on the counter. Every cent of money she had. "This is for the car."

His face brightened. "Well. Well. I see you do have some money after all."

She slid the receipt and release onto the counter and handed him a pen. "Sign this."

"What is it?"

"It's a receipt for the car. If you don't sign it, I stop payment on the check."

Without a second's hesitation, he leaned down and signed the receipt.

She scooped it up and shoved it in her purse. "That's it." She sucked in a breath. This *was* it. Get him out of her life now or spend the rest of her life worried, running. "Seriously it. That's what I was paid for tutoring Jack. I have no more money."

"Well, now, baby girl. Missy made something of herself and you're the one with the college education. You can probably do twice what she did."

Anger rumbled up in the pit of her belly. Sharp and hot, it filled her blood, raced through her veins. He had every intention of using her!

She looked at her dad. He was older than he had been, but that didn't faze her as much as the fact that he was a man, picking on a girl—his own daughter. He wasn't just scum. For the first time in her life she also saw he was a coward.

"If you ever even try to contact me again, I will call the police."

He slapped the check against his palm. "Yeah. Sure. Fine."

"I'm serious." Part of her wanted to yell. The other part was suspiciously calm. She walked around the counter, stood in front of him, feeling a power she'd never felt before. "When I file for a restraining order, I won't just tell the police you beat us. I'll air every piece of dirty linen this family has."

"Now, baby girl…"

"Don't baby girl me. I'll tell the police how you threw bleach at us when we got out of reach of your fists. I'll tell them that you broke my arm. I'll tell them how you used to burn our clothes, blacken mom's eyes, break her ribs and refuse to take her to the hospital."

He took a pace back.

He was afraid. Not of her but of the truth.

She could have said more. She could have said so much more. But he'd cost her Clark. He'd cost her the kids. Even confident that he'd never come near her again, she couldn't go back to the family she'd come to love. She didn't even know how to be in a normal family, forget about being a wife or mom.

She strode out the diner door.

Once again, she was alone on Christmas Eve.

Clark paced his office, waiting for an hour or so to pass so he could call Missy. He had absolutely no idea why Althea had felt she could or should leave…except that she was trying to protect him and his family from her father. It was skewed logic at best, but a man who'd spent three years refusing to get a DNA test for his daughter could understand. Sometimes fear of possibilities was so strong that a person couldn't see the obvious.

He walked to the window, saw the snowman and scrubbed his hand across his face. He remembered her determination to beat him in the snowball battle. He could see her butt in the air as she rolled the big snowball to make the middle of her snowman. He could feel her submission when he kissed her cold face.

The wonder of it filled him again.

He could not let her go.

He would not let her go.

The hell with waiting!

He raced out of the room, grabbed his coat. "Mrs. Alwine! I'm leaving for a few hours. Can you watch the kids?"

Althea got in her car and headed out of town. But as the sun began to rise, pale beams hit the silvery tinsel that shivered in the light breeze and it winked at her.

She blew out a relieved laugh. She'd done it. She'd faced her dad. She'd paid her debt like an honest woman and she'd faced her dad.

She wanted so much to tell Clark. She wanted to grab his shoulders and kiss his face and tell him she'd faced her demon just as she'd forced him to face his.

And wouldn't that be embarrassing? Because after she kissed him she'd have to admit that she didn't have the normal life experience to be in a family. She hadn't even had the common sense to realize they'd gone shopping for *her* the day before. Worse, she hadn't had the common sense to take the kids shopping for a gift for their dad.

Her life had been so screwed up there was no

hope for her. And she wouldn't tie him to her. After the holidays, he could walk out into the street and realize there was a whole world of women out there. And he'd find someone who wasn't scarred. Someone who knew how to be a mom. Somebody really pretty, who'd make a good hostess.

Her foot eased up on the gas pedal. Sadness trembled through her and she began to cry.

Her life sucked and—damn it—she wasn't spending another Christmas Eve alone.

She swung her car down a street that would take her to her grandmother's old house. She raced into the driveway, parking behind the humongous RV, and shoved the gearshift into Park.

She didn't consider the time. The kitchen lights were on. At least one of them was up. She pounded up the back porch steps and knocked on the door.

When Missy opened it, she fell into her arms.

"Hey. Hey!" Missy soothed. "What's up?"

"I talked to Dad."

"Oh."

"Damn it! I don't care about that."

Missy pushed her out of their embrace. "That's

even better. It's about time you shook off his hold." She frowned. "So why are you crying?"

"I left Clark."

"Oh, honey. Why?"

"I fell in love with him and the kids…and the big dog."

"Oh. Oh." She pulled her into the house. Lainie, Claire, Owen and Wyatt sat at a long black kitchen table. New cupboards had been installed. Granite countertops. Hardwood floors. And the wall that had once separated the kitchen from the rest of the house was gone.

She took a few steps toward the huge living space. Leather sofas sat in front of a stone fireplace currently decorated with five red stockings. Thick area rugs defined conversation spaces with comfortable-looking chairs. A huge Christmas tree sat in front of a wall of windows on the far side of the room. Lights and shiny ornaments twinkled at her.

She swallowed. "Wow."

Missy smiled at Wyatt. "We like it."

Her sister had everything she needed. Everything they'd both always wanted.

Fresh tears threatened to erupt.

Wyatt sprang from his seat. "Why don't I make the French toast while you two go and have a chat?"

"I don't want a chat." She wanted to be loved. She wanted to be able to love. Was that so much to ask?

"Yeah, but maybe you need a chat," Missy said, leading her toward the leather sofas just as someone knocked on the front door. "Now who the hell could that be?"

Althea's first thought was that it was their dad. But instead of fear racing through her or even anger, she merely felt tired. If he wanted her to tell him to take a hike one more time, she'd happily do so.

Her shoulders straightened. "I've got this."

Missy said, "What?" and tried to catch her as she marched through the big room to the front door, but Althea was too fast for her.

She reached the door, yanked it open and said, "What? You didn't understand what I said this morning?"

But it wasn't her dad on the front porch. It was Clark, who simply frowned. "Actually, I didn't."

Her heart about leaped out of her chest. "Clark."

"Teagan talked."

The wonder in his voice made her smile. She'd felt that same wonder the night before for the little girl they both loved. "I know. She asked me to give her pigtails last night." Her face reddened. Last night when she was sneaking out.

He shoved his hands in his jeans pockets. "Why'd you go?"

"I had to face my dad."

He reached inside the door and caught her arm. "Come on. If you want to face your dad, we'll do it now. Together."

"I already talked to him."

"Sheesh, woman. Give me ten minutes to catch up. I wanted to go with you. To help you like you helped me."

"Oh." Her pounding heart slowed. His being here was payback. "Well, thanks for the offer but I handled it."

"Really?"

"Yeah. I just stood up to him." And saying that made her feel strong again. She desperately wanted to share this with Clark, but as a mate… not some guy who thought he owed her. And she already knew she couldn't be his mate. She didn't know how. But she wouldn't embarrass herself by telling him that. She straightened her shoulders. "I'm sure you've got better things to do on a Christmas Eve morning than stand on a cold porch." Tears threatened again. She loved him. *Loved him.* Crazy dog. Adorable kids. Scruffy beard and all. If she didn't soon get away from him she'd throw herself into his arms and beg. And she was done begging. What she really wanted, what she *needed* was somebody who could accept her as she was. She started to close the door. "So, Happy Christmas."

He shoved his foot in the door. "Wait!"

She lifted her chin. "What?"

"I know these past couple of weeks have meant something to you. Don't you want to spend Christmas with me and the kids? Remember, we were making the perfect family Christmas?"

An arrow hit her in the chest. "You have Mrs. Alwine back."

"And I pay her handsomely to make Christmas dinner. I want you with us."

She shook her head. "I can't come back."

"Why not?"

She shifted to close the door again. "I'll be sharing Christmas with my family."

He lodged his foot more securely on the threshold. "I thought we were your family."

Her lips trembled and she couldn't help the words that came out of her mouth. "I thought you were, too."

His voice softened with confusion. "So why won't you come home with me?"

She would not spell it out. It was embarrassing enough that she knew she couldn't be what he needed. She refused to say it.

Refused to beg him to accept her as she was. "Goodbye, Clark."

"Goodbye? You make us love you and then you leave?"

Her gaze sprang to his. "You love me?"

"Well, yeah." He ran his hand along his neck. "I know I've been preoccupied. But I also didn't want to scare you." He winced. "It always seems like I'm pushing you into something you don't want because I'm so needy."

Oh, if he only knew she was so much better with people who were in trouble. It was people who were normal that she couldn't handle. "I'm not what you need. I don't know how to be a mom. I'm not even sure how to be a good girl-friend."

"I don't want you for a girlfriend. I want you for a wife." He stepped closer. "And as for not being what I need?" He laughed. "Who the hell knows what they really need? You're what I want. You make me laugh. You love my kids. You renamed my dog." He smiled. "That took some gumption."

She laughed, but she quickly sobered. "I pan-icked when you left to buy gifts yesterday. Two days away from Christmas and I didn't think gifts. I thought you were dropping me."

His voice softened. "Why would I drop you?"

Her lips trembled. "No one's ever really wanted me."

"We want you. A lot."

"Well, you should have let me finish. Because no one's ever wanted me I don't know how to be-have with people who do."

"Technically, no one's ever wanted me, either." Her gaze ambled to his.

"You're my first real love." He patted his stom-ach. "The one who gets me here." He touched his heart. "And here. So I don't know any more about love than you do. We'll learn together."

"You won't care if I forget the laundry?"

"We have Mrs. Alwine for laundry. I want you to love me."

Her trembling lips stilled. Tears fell off her eyelids.

"And you want me to love you?"

She nodded. "Yes."

"Well, I do." He waited a second then said, "And you love me, too?"

She nodded again.

He growled. "Say it."

She raised her head slowly, met his gaze. Staring into his pretty amber eyes she swallowed. He loved her. She loved him. She'd taken a chance with her dad. Maybe she should take the greatest risk of all? "I love you."

He scooped her into his arms and kissed her thoroughly. The way she'd seen handsome men in the movies kiss their leading ladies. Their mouths fused, their tongues danced. Happiness bubbled through her, eradicating her paralyzing fear until she couldn't even remember she'd been afraid.

When he pulled away, she clung to his jacket

collar, never wanting to let him go. Someone who knew her past and present wanted to be part of her future.

"If you guys wouldn't mind coming inside, Wyatt's got French toast."

Althea laughed through her tears. "I think we should go home to the kids."

"They'll be fine with Mrs. Alwine for a few hours."

She peeked at him.

"This time they're wrapping gifts."

She frowned, but he squeezed her shoulders. "Give you one or two Christmases and you'll catch on to all this silliness."

"I don't think it's silliness." She smiled. "I think it's magical."

Missy happily led them down the hall. "Why don't you guys come to our house tomorrow for Christmas Day?"

"Why don't you come to our house?" Clark countered. "Mrs. Alwine's baking a ham. My mom brings a turkey."

"Sounds fun." Missy said, "I'll make a cake."

Althea caught her bottom lip between her teeth.

"I hate to have Mrs. Alwine work all Christmas Day for us."

"Oh, she doesn't. She just puts the ham in the oven. My mom and I take over after that."

"In that case," Missy said, "I'll also bring a loaf of bread and maybe a salad."

"Hey, salad is my department," Wyatt said as they walked up to the table.

"I can bring cookies," Claire announced, pointing to the cooling cookies on the cooking island.

Althea stood back, watching it all, feeling the love, but most of all basking in a sense of belonging. Of family. She'd finally have the family Christmas she always wanted.

EPILOGUE

THAT SUMMER, CLARK and Althea honeymooned at a hotel Wyatt owned on the Gulf coast of Florida. Lying on a hammock, drinking pink drinks served in tall glasses, garnished with pineapple, Clark couldn't have been happier.

Althea, however, nervously sat up. "Do you think the kids are okay?"

"Spending four days with my parents at Disney World? Sheesh, woman, how much more okay could two kids get?"

She cuddled against him, then sprang up again. "Did we pack Teagan's bear?"

"If I remember correctly Teagan packed an entire bear suitcase. Something she wouldn't have been able to do without Wyatt's private plane."

"It is handy to have a rich guy for a brother-in-law."

Clark feigned offense. "Hey. I don't do so badly in the money department."

She laughed. "No. You don't."

"What? Do I have to buy you a hotel or an airplane to prove it?"

She smiled shyly and looked down. He caught her chin and lifted her face again. "What?"

"It's just all so unreal sometimes."

"What? The money? The fact that you were suddenly a mother?" He waggled his eyebrows. "Or me?"

She smiled. "You. I never ever thought I'd find somebody who would love me."

He laughed, tightened his arm around her and snuggled down in the hammock. "What are you complaining about? I didn't even know what love was."

"But we make it work."

His eyes drooped. "Every day."

She snuggled against him. "Are we really going to nap?"

"Yep."

"Nothing else on your mind?"

"Not while I'm sitting beside a hotel pool with a hundred spectators. But just wait till we get back to the honeymoon suite. Then I'm going to—" He whispered a suggestion in her ear that made her

gh. And he settled into the hammock again.
loved her laugh. Loved making her laugh.
was so warm and open and honest he knew
could make her laugh forever.

And that was the point.

* * * * *

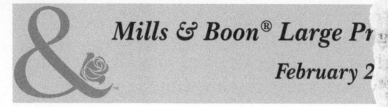

Mills & Boon® Large Pr...
February 2...

THE GREEK'S MARRIAGE BARGAIN
Sharon Kendrick

AN ENTICING DEBT TO PAY
Annie West

THE PLAYBOY OF PUERTO BANÚS
Carol Marinelli

MARRIAGE MADE OF SECRETS
Maya Blake

NEVER UNDERESTIMATE A CAFFARELLI
Melanie Milburne

THE DIVORCE PARTY
Jennifer Hayward

A HINT OF SCANDAL
Tara Pammi

SINGLE DAD'S CHRISTMAS MIRACLE
Susan Meier

SNOWBOUND WITH THE SOLDIER
Jennifer Faye

THE REDEMPTION OF RICO D'ANGELO
Michelle Douglas

BLAME IT ON THE CHAMPAGNE
Nina Harrington

0114 Rom LP

lau
He
Sh
h